U0938957

Yun Guanqiu

A crude rock washed and honed by
the tides of time,
of which each poem in this anthology
is a unique facet.

云关秋

一块被岁月的潮水洗涤和磨砺过的拙石，
本书的每首诗都是一个独特的切面。

STARLIGHT BEYOND THE MILKY WAY

【中英双语版】

银河之外的星光

云关秋◎著

张剑　赵冬◎译

中国出版集团
中 译 出 版 社

图书在版编目（CIP）数据

银河之外的星光 ：汉英对照 / 云关秋著 ；张剑，赵冬译. -- 北京 ：中译出版社，2022.9
ISBN 978-7-5001-7181-2

Ⅰ. ①银… Ⅱ. ①云… ②张… ③赵… Ⅲ. ①诗集—中国—当代—汉、英 Ⅳ. ①I227

中国版本图书馆 CIP 数据核字（2022）第 160009 号

银河之外的星光
YINHE ZHI WAI DE XINGGUANG

出版发行：中译出版社
地　　址：北京市西城区新街口外大街 28 号普天德胜大厦主楼 4 层
电　　话：010-68359719
邮　　编：100088
电子邮箱：book@ctph.com.cn
网　　址：www.ctph.com.cn

总 策 划：刘志则　　监　　制：曾荣东
策划编辑：刘春玲　　责任编辑：张　旭
文字编辑：张程程　　特约编辑：林雅宁
特约审校：钱屏匀　　营销推广：周莹莹
封面设计：方与圆　　版式设计：苏洪涛

印　　刷：艺堂印刷（天津）有限公司
经　　销：新华书店
规　　格：880 毫米 ×1230 毫米　1/32
印　　张：8
字　　数：128 千字
版　　次：2022 年 9 月第 1 版
印　　次：2022 年 9 月第 1 次

ISBN　978-7-5001-7181-2　　　定价：69.90 元

云关秋

思考者——笃行者——记述者

用最爱的文字 描绘生命之美

Yun Guanqiu

Thinker, doer and narrator

Depicting life's beauty in beloved words

目　录
Contents

【Episode Two】Experiencing the Universe in the Life of a Tree

【第二季】把一棵树活成宇宙

【Episode Four】The Horizon Always Following Behind

【第四季】身后总有地平线

【Episode One】

Billions of Stars Following You

【第一季】

亿万星辰跟你走

Starlight Beyond the Milky Way

The stars alone are the distant land of mine
Lofty mountains of those stars
Are elder brothers of my prime
Mighty rivers of those lands
Are the flowing thoughts of mine

The stars alone are the distant land of mine
Forests and oceans
Are my courtyards and pastures fine
Gallant horses on routes
Are galloping across my bosom in a line

The stars alone are the distant land of mine
The distant starlight beyond the Milky Way
O unattainable even in dreams, for which eternally I pine
Is none other than our native land—
The starting point, the finishing line.

Drafted at noon on February 1, 2019

Revised on the morning of March 30, 2020

银河之外的星光

只有群星 才是我的远方
那些地球上的高山 都是我壮年的兄长
那些大陆上的江河 都是我流淌的思想

只有群星 才是我的远方
那些森林和海洋 都是我的庭院和牧场
那些马匹 还有道路 都穿行在我的胸膛

只有群星 才是我的远方
遥不可及的遥远 银河之外的星光
梦不能至的无垠 那些永恒的未达啊
——我们出发的原乡

2019 年 2 月 1 日午 12 时初稿

2020 年 3 月 30 日晨修订

Soulmates

I have two eternal soul mates
One is sitting in the temple court
The other is slumbering in the field
One is questioning the starry resort
The other is begging food from the land

I have two eternal soul mates
One is lifting praying hands on the clouds
The other is swimming naked in the rivers
One is silent as a rock in the crowds
The other sings like a hurricane sending shivers

I have two eternal soul mates
One is thousand-faced and thousand-formed
The other is without a trace or form
One enjoys all sufferings transformed
The other plants seeds of joy as a norm.

January 8, 2020

知　音

我有两个永恒的知音
一个在庙堂端坐　一个在田间酣睡
一个向星空发问　一个向大地乞食

我有两个永恒的知音
一个在云端合掌　一个在江河裸游
一个如岩石般沉默　一个似飓风般歌唱

我有两个永恒的知音
一个有千面千相　一个却无形无踪
一个乐享所有的苦难　一个播撒粒粒的欢喜

2020 年 1 月 8 日

South of the South

North of the north
South of the south
I meditate with eyes shut
My mind reaches the farthest planet

An autumn breeze kisses the lake
That has no ripples to make
I expect the snowy winter days
Chilled to the bones, I still bask with May rays

Rolling over the river bridge
Time's wheels at every instant freeze
In a season of receding warmth
I quietly admire the cold tide winding south

Each change of the season
Is a eulogy of life for no reason
With no need for the cover of a mask
The meandering rivers south of the south have nothing to ask.

November 25, 2019

南方以南

北国之北
南方以南
合眸禅定
比遥迢更遥 比远方更远

秋风掠过的湖面
涟漪就是安然
期待冬雪的日子
凉彻入骨 且作人间五月天

车轮碾过了江桥
永恒 定格在每个瞬间
暖意退却的季节
静静欣赏 寒潮蜿蜒向南

每次季节的变幻
都是对生命的咏叹
不需要面具的遮掩
南方以南 众江迤逦不言

2019 年 11 月 25 日

Sea Walk

Braving the wind, extending both hands
Between my arms is the sand glass
And inhaling the sea gusts
I seem to have gulped all the waves

I walk alone on the sea
Swaying to the tune of marching troops
Thunderous waves are roaring in front of me
The stars with droopy heads are slumbering in groups

Treading the waves into the happy instant
Of merging the sea and the sky
Riding the wind, singing loud, caressing
The primordial forehead of the deity
All can be as small as returning to their origin
Tiny in the vast space as a sigh
All can be as great as a grain of sand
In the boundless ocean, from nonbeing to being.

June 12, 2019

踏海行

逆风而行 撑开双手
双臂之间 就是时间的沙漏
深吸一口 那劲吹的海风
仿佛把骇浪 全吞入咽喉

一个人 在海面行走
摇摆成 千军万马的节奏
涛声雷滚 眼前尽是排浪
仰目向天 众星酣睡垂首

踏浪而行 触入天海的合欢刹那
御风长歌 轻抚老神的亘古额头
渺小为 万物归元 穹间微叹
强大到 沧海一沙 从无到有

2019 年 6 月 12 日

Setting out

I am used to setting out
Yet unaccustomed to arrival
Fatigue flees me while I'm on route
Weariness greets me at the end of travel
Arrival is a kind of easy stagnation
Departure is a type of heavy elegance
I walk and stop at any station
Mountains and rivers answer with resonance.

1998

出　发

习惯出发
不习惯到达
走着的时候不觉得累
停顿下来才感到疲乏
到达是一种轻松的悲滞
出发是一种沉重的潇洒
就这样走走停停
万水千山已在我们脚下

1998 年

Beijing at 0℃

When Beijing is at zero, the color of night is dimmed
Outside the window snowflakes fly, without a sound
Afar, the aurora of orange lanterns is brimmed
When Bcijing is at zero, the feeling of drunkenness runs around
Upward the air flows, and carries free will
Downward the water sweeps, and becomes crystal still

When Beijing is at zero, black contrasts with white
Heaven and earth reach the middle game
One set piece suggests a plan well-thought
When Beijing is at zero, its soft snow and breeze does claim
Mr. Elephant overlooks all on the white hill
Miss Melody on the Long Street raises her voice solemn.

January 6, 2020

零度的北京

零度的北京 夜色朦胧
隔窗飘雪无声
远方串串橘灯
零度的北京 醉意横生
向上是任性的流动
向下是坚凝的冰晶

零度的北京 黑白分明
天地棋至中局
落子成竹在胸
零度的北京 和雪微风
象兄在白山上俯瞰
音妹在长街旁肃声

2020 年 1 月 6 日

Passing

The pendulum of time swings back and forth
All alone I have to walk on henceforth
Passing numerous cities and villages
Passing some fairies and gods
Passing countless meadows
Passing clouds of four seasons
Passing roads and intersections
Passing folks — in multitudes

Undaunted by the turbulent waves
An array of seabirds sing a low hymn
Fleeting across sequences, limits and inequations
Fleeting across poetry, fiction and prose
Fleeting across birth, nirvana and samsara
Fleeting across fright and fear in strenuous seeking
Fleeting across storm,gale and lightning
Eventually, I rest at the land of pacified mind.

January 1, 2019

过

在时光的钟摆下
一个人单独行进
路过了很多城市 和乡村
路过了一些精灵 和众神
路过了无数的草地
路过了四季的幻云
路过了道路 和路口
路过了 那么多 路上的人

在波涛的汹涌中
海鸟们列阵低吟
掠过了数列极限 不等式
掠过了诗歌小说 和散文
掠过了出生涅槃的轮回
掠过了惊恐畏惧的苦寻
掠过了暴雨 狂风 和闪电
停留在 那一方 静止的寸心

2019 年 1 月 1 日

Return

Years have gone by since I left
Time slips my mind as I drift away
In season of fairy tales reappearing
The white iceberg emerging on the surface of the bay

Returning clouds amaze with drizzling shadows
Returning seeds embrace with dazzling fruits
Returning evening breeze brings summer warmth
Returning days restart an andante in singing flutes

Let my heart dash through the empty streets
Despite the long journey, my soul is still young and revived
My hands gently touch the aspen trees' tender pleats
This very day, month and year witness my life relived.

July 7, 2019

归 来

已经离开了很多很多年
渐行渐远 忘记了时间
在童话的季节里 重新出现
洁白的冰山 浮出水面

归来的云朵 以雨丝的身影惊艳
归来的种子 以果实的面孔斑斓
归来的晚风 带来初夏的温暖
归来的岁月 重启如歌的行板

让心灵 飞奔在空无一人的小街
此行漫漫 魂兮归来 依旧是少年
用双手 轻抚白杨林的鬓边
此后种种 重生在今年 今月 今天

2019 年 7 月 7 日

Afar

I thought my feet had measured a long road
Yet in fact, all is but a blink in time, a change in mind
The farthest place is not over mountains or horizons

I thought deeds were mightier than words
Yet eventually, words is deeds, and deeds denote words
Profound words are beyond the mouth and the throat

The emptiness my fingers touch
Is the truthfulness of truth
Somewhere in my heart
Is the distantness of distance.

May 1, 2018

远　方

曾经以为双脚走了很久
其实只是光阴一瞬　心念一转
最远的路　不在山外天边

曾经以为行胜于言
到头来言即是行　行亦是言
最深的话　不在嘴角喉间

用手指触碰的虚空
那是真实的真
在心灵的某个角落
那是远方的远

2018 年 5 月 1 日

Resisting

In the wilderness of a cold winter
I hear myself like internodes growing and crackling
Facing all darkness alone
I am ready for

Resisting all adversities
What I need most is not strength, but will
In moments of hesitation and frustration
Grant us persistence, not desperation.

1997

抵　抗

在寒冬的旷野上
我听见 自己在噼里啪啦地拔节生长
即使面对所有的黑暗
一个人也可以进行抵抗

对抗逆境
最需要的 常常是意志 而不是力量
在犹豫与动摇的时刻
让我们坚持 而不是忧伤

1997 年

Hand Me the Towline

In falling drizzles I was born in the south
Among sorghums I grow in the north
Passing down the fairy lanes sparkling with stars
Wading the autumn rivers with torrential waters
Today I stand on the mountain pass, defying the blast
And declaring to the world: I've matured at last

Are they boundless forests that around my lips grow?
Are they towering mountains that from my Adam's apple arise?
O land of the north and south, on me your personality you bestow

A man true not every man is
To find the pyramid in my heart
I set the sun sails, and start the arduous exploration
Braving wind and snow, over mountains and deserts
Let time mold me into an everlasting statue
I shall bring no shame to my sonorous gender and golden skin

给我纤索

同南方的细雨一起 诞生了我
同北方的高粱一起 生长了我
穿过嵌着星星的 童话的小巷
涉过山洪澎湃的 秋天的河
今天 我站在了吹鼓着强风的山口
向整个世界宣布 我 长大了

我唇边长起的 是无尽的森林吗
我喉头突起的 是巍峨的山峦吗
北方南国的土地啊 你给了我 你自己的性格

并非男子汉 就是每一个男子
为了心中的金字塔
我扬起太阳帆 走向艰难的开拓
走向朔风和白雪 走向高山和大漠
让岁月 把我化成 一座永恒的雕塑
我将无愧于 我响亮的性别 我金黄的肤色

I will grow, singing a slightly hoarse yet bold song
My heart will be the blue sky after rain, wide and long
I will age, and my back will arch as a mountain strong
Haply, I may dream of the birch at the gate of my village
Upon which perches a kite, after the white pigeon flying
Yet my last line will not be a tender sigh like a falling leaf
For I've had the world and lived a true life without grief

Methinks I saw, drifting up in the night sky, clouds of mum's sorrows
Methinks I saw Helios' Chariot pulling dad's heavy towline
Mum, please confide to me all your deep sorrows
And dad, hand me, hand me — the long towline.

October 19, 1984

我将成熟 将会唱起一支略带沙哑的 粗犷的歌
只要我的心 永远像雨后的蓝天 深远而辽阔
我会衰老 我的背 会像山脉一样隆起
也许 我会想起 家乡门前的那株白桦
白桦树上栖落的风筝 风筝追逐着的白鸽
可我的最后一句话 不会是落叶般的叹息
因为我曾拥有整个世界 因为我曾属于真正的生活

仿佛见 暗色的夜空中 飘着妈妈忧虑的云朵
仿佛见 太阳之车啊 牵引着父亲沉重的纤索
妈妈啊 告诉我 把你的忧虑告诉我
父亲啊 给我 给我——纤索

1984 年 10 月 19 日

Truth

The truth does not loaf about the streets
The fact ne'er flows around the lips
Burnt in the heart, enthusiasm moved only me
Yet all is lamentation on deceased youth or eclipsed angle

The first half of my life is committed to memory
The mature age initiates learning to forget
Seek gracefully a most beautiful angle
To depict the fond illusions with which my mind is beset

The vanity greater than the greatest
The invisibility tinier than the tiniest
Is incarnated with a new dimension of fate
Folded into a surface, singing with refrains shiny

Carve each instant into eternity
Dissolve every minute into aroma
Ne'er seek the truth of eternity
That hides itself in quiet soma.

September 21, 2019

真

真理 常常不在街上 游荡
真相 往往不在嘴边 流淌
曾经满腔热血 只是感动了自己
竟是青春的伤逝 或角度的虚晃

前半生 苦苦练习铭记
不惑年 开始学习遗忘
优雅地寻找 一个最美的角度
去描绘自己喜欢的那些幻象

比最大 更大的重重虚妄
比最小 更小的若现若藏
跨越一个维度 再次重生
拼折一个曲面 循环歌唱

把每一刻 都刻成永恒
让每一分 都分解馨香
不要寻找 永恒的真意
它们需要安静地躲藏

2019 年 9 月 21 日

Mountain Range

Never will a man see
The falling of a mountain range
In the dense fog will they
Erase their quiet shapes

Rare is it to hear
The myths of those mountains
Their legends, flowing on the bosom, pleasing to the ear
Belong to another people.

January 15, 2021

山 脉

永远 也不会 看到
一座山脉的 倒下
他们 只是 在浓雾中
悄悄地 归隐

很难 听得到 那些
关于山脉的 神话
他们的 胸膛 流淌的动听
传说 属于另一群人

2021 年 1 月 15 日

Taking-off

The moment I am about to leave the ground
My heart is feeling intense pulsations
Though I eventually will be earth bound
I still aim at flying up into the blue sky
Though pressure sends tingling to my ear drum
Flying is still the greatest yearning I never recover from.

1999

起　飞

在离开大地的瞬间
心灵感受到了剧烈的震颤
明知终将返回地面
可我们还是要飞向蓝天
尽管压力刺痛了耳膜
飞翔依旧是最大的心愿

1999 年

The Topmost

Standing on the topmost
Is pressing my chest tightly to the ground
To let each heart-beat
Echo with the breath of the soil

Standing on the topmost
Is letting my feet grow root strands
To let eons of longings at their utmost
Touch the blurred groundwater

Drifting clouds high in the sky
Fall as rain, permeating the earth
Noble souls from the Most High
Descend as dust, becoming roadbeds with mirth

The lowest my heart knows
Is the topmost.

March 6, 2019

最高处

站在最高处
就是把胸膛紧贴着 大地
让每一声心跳
去共鸣 泥土的呼吸

站在最高处
就是让双脚生长出 根须
任千百万思念
去触摸 地下水的迷离

高天的云朵
化雨 融入大地
高贵的灵魂
变土 幻为路基

心在最低
这最高的矗立

2019 年 3 月 6 日

Lead

Lead the wind along
The clouds will follow you
Lead the clouds along
The trees will follow you
Lead the trees along
The mountains will follow you
Lead the mountains along
All the earth will follow you

Lead Time's threads along
Billions of stars will follow you
Lead the billions of stars along
Eternal Time's torrents will follow you.

February 7, 2021

牵

牵着风
云会跟你走
牵着云
树会跟你走
牵着树
山会跟你走
牵着山
整个大陆跟你走

牵着漫漫的时间线
亿万星辰跟你走
牵着亿万星辰
永恒的时间 逐你奔流

2021 年 2 月 7 日

Growth Rings

1985

On land and over the sea
If truth and hope can't be found
Then, the grand two
E'en in heaven won't be around

1999

On the broad road slowly you walk
On the boundless plain you won't advance
Why let thousand excuses your way block
You know that mediocrity is not plainness

2002

Regard each of your fall
As a chance to stand tall.

年 轮

1985

如果陆地和海洋

不存在真理和希望

那么 它们

注定 也不在天上

1999

宽阔的路上 你走得很慢

一马平川 却止步不前

何必 为自己寻找借口

要知道 平庸不是平淡

2002

把每一次跌倒

都当成 更高站立的契机

The Past of the Future

To All That's Happened and Will Happen

From the bottom of the sea, the rock
Slowly starts to rise and hump up
We have seen the end that's in stock
People stand under its feet, and name it Peak Rock
(To the 1990s)

If life could be fictional fantasy
I will choose to give up each contingency
And wish each detail to happen with certainty
As my bare feet step on rocks totally
(To the first decade of the 21st century)

Those marathon races of mine
I'll complete with a young spine
To my youth, eighty years I assign
(To the second decade of the 21st century)

Tree planters tell tree stories
Mansion builders tell mansion stories
Story-livers never tell stories
Those who love to tell stories
Only tell others' stories.
(To the 2020s)

April 18, 2021

未来的往事

——致已经和即将发生的

这块石头 沉在海底
在挤压之下 慢慢隆起
我们看到了 最后的结局
人们 站在它的脚下 称之为峰石
（致 20 世纪 90 年代）

如果人生可以虚构
我还是放弃 所有的偶然
让每个细节 都必然发生
行走的赤足 全踩在石上
（致 21 世纪第一个十年）

我的那些马拉松
将在少年时 跑完
我的少年时光 横跨八十年
（致 21 世纪第二个十年）

种树的人 讲 树的故事
建楼的人 讲 楼的故事
能讲故事的人 不讲故事
爱讲故事的人
讲的都是 别人的故事
（致 21 世纪 20 年代）

2021 年 4 月 18 日

【Episode Two】

Experiencing the Universe in the Life of a Tree

【第二季】

把一棵树活成宇宙

Lake Romance

The days when I am beside you
I sense that mysterious attention
And I hear, from afar, and near my ear too
The aroma, the breath of a deity.

The days when you are not at my side
I still hear the melody cold and clear
And behold, flowing across the sky with pride
The rhythm dear to a god's ear.

There is no need to seek on purpose
The half-hidden miracles at the lakeside
In the light clouds, with the breeze, it gathers and disperses
In lakes, by green banks, it is surrounded on all sides

Eyes shut, the lake in the sky; eyes closed, you in my arms
With tears in palms, I have no fear in heart
Either you remain in the twilight with beaming charms
Or homeward you go, in the tender ripples which part.

January 4, 2021

湖　恋

在你的身边
感受到了 那种隐秘的注意
听到了 那遥远 又在耳畔的
气息 那就是神的呼吸

离开你的日子
还能听到 那些清冽的旋律
还看见 那高天 流淌过的
节奏 那就是神的欢喜

不用刻意 寻找
湖畔 似隐似现的 神迹
在薄云里 随微风 散聚
在湖水中 被绿岸 围起

合眸 空中有湖 闭目 怀中有你
掌中有泪 心无余戚
不在绚丽的 夕阳下 旖旎
就在轻柔的 涟漪中 归去

2021 年 1 月 4 日

The World

Far have years gone away
Over the spotless clean you can never hold sway
The purest things of the day
Are not in the world to stay

Instill black graphite into white oak juice
Flexible wheels can roll over any causeway
In fragile crude iron, from carbon bravely break away
Turn iron into steel, and the dignity of metal will weigh

Inclusive or exclusive
All mature trees have dappled faces.

2000

人　间

岁月遥远
不要追求一尘不染
那些纯而又纯的东西
不在人间

在洁白的橡汁中加入黑色的石墨
柔韧的车轮能碾过各种路面
在脆弱的生铁中勇敢脱碳
化铁为钢方显金属的尊严

包容　或者　扬弃
成熟的树　都有一张斑驳的脸

2000 年

Awakening Insects

It is the calling of the sky thunder
It is the banishment by the earth fire
Split open the cave with my hands; step into the dark on my feet
The longer I walk on the road, the brighter is the sky
Not far away in the distance, the crouching spring I espy

Those long years of patient forbearance
Beside countless painful miseries beyond tolerance
I cannot yell it out, nor can I swallow it
Listening, in silence, to my thumping heart-beat
That is the long-held declaration of the hermit

Dissolve myself into melting rivers, surging forward
Ride the mild wind, to the thousand passes northward
Hovering with passion, whirling without restraint
I lift my eyes to meet the gigantic eyes in firmament
O that is my home bound instant in tacit agreement.

March 3, 2020, the date of Awakening Insects

惊　蛰

是天雷的召唤
是地火的驱赶
用双手扒开洞口　让双脚踏入黑暗
路越走　天就会越亮
前方不远处　就蹲伏着春天的温暖

那么长的隐忍岁月
还有无法计数的苦痛磨难
吼不出来　无法吞咽
沉默聆听　自己一声声沉沉的心跳
那是蛰伏者积蓄已久的宣言

融入解冻的江河　一起奔涌
拥抱温婉的长风　北上千关
纵情掠过　肆意飞旋
抬头对望　苍穹一双双深邃的巨眼
那是归去来兮的默契瞬间

2020 年 3 月 3 日　惊蛰之日

When the Storm Rages

When the storm rages
My arms dance like waving branches
My feet stand firm like tree roots

When the storm rages
My body runs with the blast, only swifter
My mind is calmer than the storm center

When the storm rages
I cultivate the tenacity of a blade of grass
I admire the composure of a stone.

January 25, 2020

暴风袭来的时候

暴风袭来的时候
双臂 像树枝一样舞动
双脚 像树根一样坚定

暴风袭来的时候
身体 比疾风跑得更快
心灵 比风眼还要宁静

暴风袭来的时候
修炼 一株小草的韧性
欣赏 一颗石子的从容

2020 年 1 月 25 日

Another Kind of Spring

Today is a day farther
From winter than yesterday
Tomorrow is a day closer
To spring than today
Counting the seconds, I hurt my finger tips
Waiting alone, I find time slower than snails

I confide to myself an ultimate secret
Another kind of spring needs no expecting
Quicken your running to make time spin
Catch up with spring to embrace her, together whirling
As long as your whirls to the high speed cling
You can always stay in your own spring.

April 20, 2020

还有一种春天

今天 比昨天
离寒冬 又远了一天
明天 比今天
离春天 又近了一点
数过了秒针 掰痛了指尖
孤独地等待 时间变得好慢

告诉自己 一个终极的秘密
还有一种春天 就是不再期盼
只有加速奔跑 才能让时间快转
追上了春天 就拥抱着一起飞旋
只要旋得够快 就可以
永远停留在自己的春天

2020 年 4 月 20 日

Ode

For a fall that is solemn
For a calm walk in harm's way
For an instant of warm tears on the face
For the eternity of a silent standing
By the sacred trust of Mother Earth
I wave mighty rivers, to write you an ode

For the softness under iron strength
For the firmness under panic
For the new route after despair
For the brightness above the poisonous fog
By the name of Father Mount
I wave mighty clouds, to write you an ode

For the innocence paved with purity
For the sacredness molded with red color
For the immortality carved on monuments
For the fading figure under the limelight
The grateful populace, bathing in the sunshine
Dip a brush into ink of tears, to write you an ode.

February 22, 2020

颂 歌

为了 庄严的倒下
为了 沉着的逆行
为了 泪流满面的瞬间
为了 无言矗立的永恒
我受大地母亲的重托
挥江河之笔 为你写下颂歌

为了 刚强下的柔软
为了 恐慌中的坚定
为了 绝境之后的新路
为了 迷雾以上的光明
我以高山父亲的名义
擎万云之笺 为你写下颂歌

为了 洁白铺满的纯真
为了 殷红铸就的神圣
为了 牺牲之碑铭刻的不朽
为了 聚光灯下或将淡化的身影
太阳照耀下的感恩生灵
蘸热泪之墨 为你写下颂歌

2020 年 2 月 22 日

July

With a start, I realize I owe a farewell to the spring
Already, unexpectedly, it is July
I had expected a first stroke of green
As I lift my head, lush greens in front of my eyes appear

Narrowly have I missed the long-awaited spring
The phantoms, passing abreast of me, are flickering
My clumsy hands sew warm clothes with rough stitches
Of the impending cold winter, children have not noted a thing

I deemed it a mere beginning
Already has come the month of July
I deemed it an imminent ending
Actually in sight is the month of July.

July 5, 2019

七　月

忽然惊觉 没有和春天告别
竟然 已是七月
原本 只期待一抹新绿
抬头间 浓翠目不暇接

擦肩错过了 期待已久的季节
穿胸而过的幻影 时现时灭
拙手缝制 粗针大线的寒衣
对将至的冷冬 孩子们浑然不觉

以为刚刚开始
竟然 已是七月
以为即将结束
其实 只是七月

2019 年 7 月 5 日

Midsummer

Ere the coming of the autumn season
I learn to trim my figure tall and upright
Like the sturdy golden grass in the storm
Or the mottled birch in chilly winter

Ere the wind blows in the autumn season
I learn to dissolve and melt a gentle temper
Like a lone goose flying south bravely
Or the subterranean rivers deeply hidden

Since that strong willed seed
Has sprouted in the spring field
That heavy body must need
This midsummer shoulders that ne'er yield

At the most magnificent instant
Inhale light and splendor from the sun
In the most scorching season
With a smile, set out, and to the cold, run.

July 20, 2019

仲 夏

在秋天到来之前
学习着让身姿 傲立挺拔
就像强风中的金黄劲草
就像寒冬里的斑驳白桦

在秋风吹来之前
练习着把温柔 消解融化
就像孤雁倔强地昂首南飞
就像暗河的水深藏地下

那颗坚强的种子
既然已经 在春天发芽
那副厚重的行囊
就必须担起 在这个仲夏

在最美丽的时刻
向着太阳 吸纳光华
在最炎热的季节
向着寒冷 微笑出发

2019 年 7 月 20 日

Fire

Have you ever lit a fire?
On the highlands remote and desolate
Drilling the hard wood, not fearing pains of hand
Only to hide the eyes of fierce wolves

Have you ever lit a fire?
In a first-class office with fire emergency showers
Not fearing to bare chests, lower so-called dignity
Only to melt glaciers in your eyes into waters

Have you ever lit a fire?
On those waste lands of the heart
Burn down thick walls, and level abysses
Only to build a road that goes far

Have you ever lit a fire?
When the firewood is used up, ignite your blood of passion
Have you ever lit a fire?
When the fire burns up, it emits the brightest warmth.

July 8, 2019

火

你 生过火吗
在杳无人迹的高原
拼命转动坚木 哪怕把双手磨烂
只为了 遮住残暴的狼眼

你 生过火吗
在布满喷淋的甲级写字间
不惧袒露襟怀 放下了所谓的身段
只为了 融化眸子里的冰川

你 生过火吗
在那些心灵的荒原
烧穿那一堵堵厚墙 填平一道道深渊
只为了 修一条道路 通向遥远

你 生过火吗
当柴草烧尽 就把热血点燃
你 生过火吗
当火光熄灭 才是最亮的温暖

2019 年 7 月 8 日

River Town in Winter Rain

Day darkens like night
Buildings at sky's end are veiled in haze
Tides of people come in sight
Underground is once again at its hasty rush

Myriad stripes of trickling, chilling rain
Are pleated into intertwined feeling
Going in the opposite direction of the multitudes
Produce fiery passions sparkling and flying

The snowless capital city
With no freezing cold blanketing the sky
Spill the feeling of spring to re-sketch the blue print
Turn the golden keys, to switch to the soundless harmony

River Town in winter rain
With crystal of courtesy in my hand
I sip the tea, bidding farewell to the past
And turning wine fervor into sounding bells.

January 12, 2020

冬雨江城

白昼如夜
天际的楼宇 眉眼蒙眬
人潮似水
地下的枢纽 行色匆匆

用亿万条冷雨
雕琢交错黏结的心境
与千百人逆向
擦出火花四溅的激情

无雪之都
没有漫天寒彻的冰冷
洒春意 重绘蓝图
转金匙 切换无言的和声

冬雨江城
手捧彬彬有礼的晶莹
饮清茶 告别往事
挥洒意 化成壮丽的钟鸣

2020 年 1 月 12 日

Snow

In days when dark clouds are hanging over
I quietly await a snow, as heavy as possible
Not light, but heavy, as weather forecasts said
My yearning, though not persistent, is enthusiastic

Come! The snow storm of my life
If in bits and pieces, then it has no flying wild ecstasy
For each round of snow I compose a poem
To eulogize each down-drifting as baptismal fantasy

Blotting out the sky, covering its eye, that is Beauty
If unable to regenerate everything, then cover everything
Even in half-disclosed beauty, it also exhibits charm
Both truth unbosomed, and icy moon bone-chilling

Come! You snows, heavy or light
Gone are the moments of the biting wind and cold night
For each round of snow in life a poem of praise I write
Into leisurely music I turn all days gloomy or bright.

At 6 pm, December 15, 2019

雪

阴云密布的日子里
静候着 一场能多大 就多大的雪
天气预报说的不小 哦很大
期待不太执着 但是有点热烈

来吧 那生命中的暴风雪
如果星星点点 就没有漫天纷扬的狂野
为每一场雪 赋一首诗
赞美每一次洗礼般的倾泻

如果遮天蔽日 该是大写的美好
不能重生一切 那就覆盖一切
如果半遮半掩 也是平凡的娇娆
既是真情吐露 也有透骨冰月

来吧 这一场场或大或小的雪
去了 那一刻刻的寒风苦夜
为生命中的每一场雪 赋一首赞美的诗
把阳光和阴郁的日子 全谱成悠然的音乐

2019 年 12 月 15 日晚 6 时

Winter Days

Winter days one by one, have to be lived
Its time hard to endure by mind is twisted and lengthened
Unlike the colorful summer spent lavishly and willfully
For the time of beauty transient is never remembered

The memory is stuffed with the so-called miseries
Having been washed and rinsed by the changing time
They suddenly, at one time, become mellowed fragrance
What you miss on the route are the leisurely bits
Until comes the day recollected by the Master
Who, from afar, fondly reflects on the past happiness

Having come in haste, winter days inch on
Carve a deep line into the growth ring
Set the ice bars crackling and clanking thereon
That is the great Tao prevailing in heaven
Who knows the instant of aloofness from the sun?
Who knows the planets' sadness, unable the sun to shun?

At noon, January 28, 2019

冬　日

冬日的时光 是一天一天过的
因为难熬 时间 被心灵 扭曲拉长
不像那绚丽的夏 可以肆意挥霍
因为美好 稍纵即逝 转瞬则忘

记忆里塞满的 恰是那所谓的苦难
经历了岁月的淘洗
在某一刻 突然变成 刻骨的醇香
一路上遗落的 是闲适的点滴
等待有一天 主人回首
把曾经的幸福 远远眺望

冬日 匆匆而来 慢慢踱过
刻一行最深的年轮之印
爆几声咔咔的冰凌撞响
大道天行
谁知 那一刻与大阳的疏远
谁解 那欲挣脱而不得的行星之殇

2019年1月28日午12时

Third Nine[1]

From Lesser Cold to Greater Cold
The Sun slants his reluctant shining smile
From First Nine to Third Nine
The Earth exhausts his cherished warmth

In south, the geese look northward, at the eighty-one perils
At the end of the Ninth Nine, spring returns to their feathers
The cold ice does not like the blandness of the spring season
Due to the Third Nine it falls in love with the cold of wintry weathers.

On January 17, 2020, the last day of the Third Nine-Day period

① Third Nine refers to the peak of the coldness, that is, the third "nine days" after Winter Solstice.

三　九

从小寒向大寒

阳光斜散着 勉强的笑颜

数一九到三九

大地耗尽了 珍存的温暖

南雁北眺 八十一磨难

九九期满 春回到羽间

坚冰不喜 春意的平淡

竟因三九 恋上了严寒

2020 年 1 月 17 日　三九最后一天

Yang

May an early sun-beam cross down space
Like the giant pillar that holds up the sky
With shining splendor. We wish this
Burning torch would
The dark disperse and the passion ignite

May there be energy fountains extracted and refined
Like a lone peak stand
Disregarding all mountains, and may this landmark
Of blossoming spring carve a New Year mark
And quicken the steps of warmth in the land

Just after the Sixth Nine, and prior to the New Year's Eve
Promptly, promptly, follow ordinances and never hesitate
Idle light waves cannot the icy surface cleave
The late warmth feels ashamed before the whole spring
When the sun stands erect, all would shine bright colors.

On the morning of February 5, 2021

阳

期待 一根 提前穿越的
大阳线 像擎天巨柱
辉煌灿烂 期待着 这把
熊熊燃烧的火炬 把
寒冷驱散 把 激情点燃

期待 一束 萃取精提的
能量源 像孤峰独立
傲视群山 期待着 这座
春意盎然的地标 刻
新年之记 促 大地回暖

就在六九之后 请在除夕之前
急急如律令 刻刻不容缓
懒散的光波 无力融解冰面
迟到的温暖 愧对整个春天
大阳挺立时 万物皆斑斓

2021 年 2 月 5 日晨

A Time for Farewell

Raise wine glasses, and let our eyes meet
Let the thousand days and nights of waiting
Be the sweet silence at this very moment
A thousand roads to us are belonging
We shall to the distant land turn our feet

Do we linger on the meadow, the green water of the pond?
Do we linger on the flickering neon-lights, the music of group dance?
Not any more, I respond
Today, the world has granted you all the space and chance
For you to soar without bond

No, let no sad tears run
Ours is every forthcoming night plated with love
Still will I play the guitar for you
You will hear, my love
The wordless song of mine to shine
With starlight, far away, far above

告别时候

举杯 我们相望
让一千多个日夜的等待
这一刻 化为沉默
有一千条大路属于我们
我们 属于远方

可还留恋那片草地 可还留恋那潭碧水
可还留恋闪烁的霓虹灯 和集体舞曲的交响
不必了
今天 世界给了你所有的空间
让你翱翔

不 不要流泪
以后的每一个镀着爱的夜晚 依旧属于我们
我的六弦琴 还会为你弹响
你会听见
我的无字的歌声
闪着遥远的星光

Stone walls shall we run into, and
Blood shall we shed, which we shall not grieve
Crystals will be waiting for us to discover alike
And soils will be waiting for us to sow—
With seeds of spring and sunshine alike

We possess the youth of twenty, which
The eye of heaven possesses
Tomorrow, we will set out for long voyage.

October 23, 1984

会有石壁的 我们要去碰撞

会流点鲜血的 但我们不会忧伤

更会有水晶 等待我们去发现

更会有土壤 等待我们去播种

——播种春天和阳光

我们拥有 二十岁的年龄

二十岁的年龄 拥有太阳的目光

明天 我们就要远航

1984 年 10 月 23 日

Spring Ballad

Spring, a drop of crystal falling
By a graceful line, falls into the fresh green
Strands of old melancholy from winter are drifting
Slowly fading away, having absorbed the sun's warmth

Reluctant departure, teary farewell
Gratification of release, pleasure of break-free
Give unto winter, the solemnity of farewell
Embrace summer rain, the yearning for telling

Spring, a drop from the river of time
With excursion footsteps, kisses the spring soil
On empty branches shall fresh leaves be growing
On the silent fields shall blossoms sway.

April 4, 2021

春 谣

春 一滴坠落的晶体
优美的流线 落入新绿
从冬天飘来的 丝丝旧郁
吸收春阳的微暖 缓缓散去

无奈的不舍 含泪的别离
释放的欣慰 挣脱的欢喜
告别的郑重 交给冬季
向往的倾诉 迎向夏雨

春 一颗时光的水滴
踏青的脚步 轻吻春泥
空荡荡的枝头 新叶将栖
原野不语 万花摇曳

2021 年 4 月 4 日

Philosophy

The roads I have traveled
The adversities I have triumphed over
Like sprouting thoughts I have yet unraveled
Or parallel world this one crosses
The unexamined mysteries
The unresolved doubts
I give a slight thought and a casual laugh

The unknown awaiting
The known desolation
The science of science, the thinking about thinking
The logic of logic, the confusion about confusion
Meaning and truth intersecting
Thus, I understand the Creator's lonesome isolation
And prefer the lovable and laughable world of the living

哲

走过的道路
穿过的坎坷
似曾萌生的思想
或有另一种平行 和这一世擦肩而过
以为透视的奥秘
还未想透的疑惑
淡淡地想想 笑笑了呵呵

未知的期待
已知的落寞
关于科学的科学 关于思索的思索
关于逻辑的逻辑 关于困惑的困惑
关于意义和真相的交织错落
理解了造物主的孤独
更喜欢可笑又可爱的人间烟火

Both Zodiac sign and profession I share with the heroic clown
For the clownish hero, I drink a little and sing in a low voice
Praise the low and worldly on which I once looked down
Let go of the vehement heat that brought blood and tears
Thus, I come; thus, I drift over the town
Experience a universe in the life of a tree
Eyes closed, I contemplate the heart's moment, and feel in bosom
a billion stars.

June 25, 2020

与英雄般的小丑 同属同行
为小丑式的英雄 浅酌低歌
赞美曾经蔑视的低俗
放下沸腾过的血泪之热
就这样来过 就这样飘过
把一棵树活成宇宙
闭眸观心之瞬 胸有亿万星河

2020 年 6 月 25 日

City

A goblet of wine is a city
The blossom of scarlet liquid is the city's heart
A book is a city
The unfathomable chapters are the city's haze
A car is a city
Outside the windows is the city's hazy suburb
A modest man is a city, magnificent and grand
The cordial smile is the city's spring sun-shine

A paragraph is a city
The momentary loss of words is the city's past
A song is a city
The splendor of the tenor voice is the city's horizon
A crowd is a city
The racing and chasing is the city's phantom
The current you is my future city
This city of mine is laying base in the valley.

On the evening of April 14, 2021

城

一杯酒 是一座城
那朵殷红的液 是城市的心
一本书 是一座城
那读不懂的篇章 是城市的雾霭
一辆车 是一座城
那窗外的懵懂 是城市的郊野
一个温润的人 是你壮阔的城
这份暖暖的微笑 是城市的春阳

一段话 是一座城
那欲言又止的忐忑 是城市的过往
一首歌 是一座城
那高音展现的华彩 是城市的天际
一群人 是一座城
那奔跑和追逐 是城市的魅影
一个当下的你 是我未来的城
这座属我的都市 正在深谷筑基

2021 年 4 月 14 日晚

Ode to the Wind of China

Riding the green bull, Lao Zi bids farewell to Hangu Pass
Riding the chariot, Confucius has his heart in the states
The benevolent utter the unutterable Tao; the sages music and rituals compose
Harmony spans the five continents; Heaven-Earth follows the Self-So
The Zhou cauldrons and the Qin bricks mold China's ethos
Tang poetry and Song Ci verse unfold in long scrolls
On the Towering Kunlun are nine peaks and heavens
For a billion years the strong wind of China blows

Wield the brush, and beacon-fires of ten thousand li die
Play the zither, and the lingering sound is like fall of pearls on jade plates
The benevolent utter the unutterable Tao; the sages music and rituals compose
Harmony spans five continents; Heaven-Earth follows the Self-So
Across seas and oceans the Silk Roads extend
The Big Dipper and stars move; Heaven's vigor eternally flows
As deep as eight thousand feet the Pacific Ocean knows
For a billion years the strong wind of China blows.

April 26, 2017

华风颂

骑青牛挥别函谷关
乘木车心在列国盘桓
仁者非常道 诸子礼乐篇
和气贯五洲 天地法自然
周鼎秦砖铸风骨
唐诗宋词谱长卷
巍峨昆仑九重山
华风劲吹亿万年

挥朱毫万里息烽烟
抚古琴余音珠落玉盘
仁者非常道 诸子礼乐篇
和气贯五洲 天地法自然
跨海越洋丝绸路
星移斗转天行健
太平洋深八千丈
华风劲吹亿万年

2017 年 4 月 26 日

Everlasting and Awe-inspiring

A Segment of an Ode to the Wisdom of Chinese Philosophy

Ocean embraces oceans
A symphony of lush yellow and vivid blue
The Milky Way crosses the sky
A Kshana of collision with eternity

Everlasting and awe-inspiring
The majestic river has winded through numerous peaks
Awe-inspiring and everlasting
The primordial starlight has illumined ancient time

From high lands to mountains, forests are continuous
That is the giant king tree, with roots infinitely spreading
From lakes to tiny cracks, the highest good is in all that grows
That is the unparalleled Tao creating all from nothing

Everlasting and awe-inspiring
Jump into the boundless sea of grand thoughts forever recurring
Awe-inspiring and everlasting
Admire the myriad statues of silent wisdom, one hand on my forehead.

November 27, 2019

悠兮壮哉

——致中华哲学智慧的片段颂歌

大洋拥抱大洋
浑黄和蔚蓝的交响
银河瞬移天际
刹那和永恒的对撞

悠兮壮哉
那穿越了万重群山的江流浩荡
壮哉悠兮
那照耀过遥远岁月的亘古星光

从高原到群山　森林连绵
那是根系无限的巨树之王
从湖泊到微隙　上善广泽
那是零生万物的大道无双

悠兮壮哉
纵身跃入　那无限循环的浩瀚思想
壮哉悠兮
只手扶额　那静水深流的万千雕像

2019 年 11 月 27 日

【Episode Three】

Tramping like Ice Melting

【第三季】

好似冰融化了去流浪

Walking on

Walking on and on, things are getting lost
Lost are commonplace ideals, or ordinary commonsense
Lost are plentiful time, and fond innocence

Walking on and on, people are getting dispersed
Like falling leaves departing autumn trees, or snowflakes melting into spring branches
Like little colts leaving the herd of horses, or the prodigal son expecting homecoming

Walking on and on, some roads are changed
Some take on what they disdained; some shoulder others' troubles
Like ice melting to wander; like water vaporing to fly

I used to walk, and now continue to walk
The vigorous walker is without worries; the happy walker knows no sense of direction.

January 9, 2020

走　着

走着走着　有的东西就丢了
譬如常见的理想　譬如平凡的常识
没了那大把的光阴　失了曾喜欢的幼稚

走着走着　有的人就散了
就像落叶告别了秋树　就像雪花融进了春枝
离开马群的幼驹　多像盼归的游子

走着走着　有的路就变了
有人担当了曾经的不屑　有人扛起了别人的心事
好似冰融化了去流浪　好似水蒸腾了去飞驰

曾经走着　继续走着
健行者没有心事　乐行者不妨路痴

2020 年 1 月 9 日

To Youth

The flaming of life
Is a game both related and unrelated
To the years you have lived

The pilot is the new falling leaf
The wick is the tree's old bark

The happiness of being brave after failure
The right of crying with no pain

Shedding the clamor of dancing against the wind
Twining passion and innocence into meaning

With a soaring zeal, let me burn
And touch the ashes with memory's fingertips

With shining pellets by the high temperature crystallized
To resist the increasing greasiness.

May 4, 2019

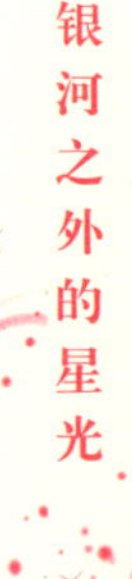

致青春

生命的火焰燃起
这与年龄
相关亦无关的游戏

引火是新发的落叶
烛心是苍老的树皮

那败而无馁的幸福
那不痛而哭的权利

洒下一路御风舞动的喧嚣
把热诚和天真拧成意义

燃烧吧 炽烈地升腾
再用回忆的指尖 抚摸满地灰絮

找到几颗高温烧结的晶体
去抵抗丝丝增长的油腻

2019年5月4日

Years of Glory

A thousand years in an instant, ten thousand in a blink
In this way let me gently gaze
At the years condensed into a cold block

On my shoulders is a stone hoe
To inscribe characters into the stone
Firm determinations will always aim at the star

Gone are the vented feelings after moderate drinking
Cherished are the restless anthems of vigorous striving
Into the melody to which no one is listening
Are incised the immortal years of glory.

In the 2000s

光辉岁月

千年一瞬 万年一瞥
就这样轻轻地眺望
时光就完成了冻结

扛一把石锄
把字写在石头上
锐志 永远不会磨灭

流失的 只是浅酌后的宣泄
留下的 是奋斗的壮歌不歇
那一段无人倾听的乐曲
刻印着不朽的光辉岁月

21 世纪

Walk to the Far-off

Here the scenes of sporty colors
Can never be my destination
There is a far-off place under the skies
Guiding the direction of my eyes

Maybe walking to the far-off
Is still not the limit ultimate
I will once again set off
Though with unsteady steps

Life is a rowing boat
The other shore is the goal.

1999

走向遥远

这里的景色斑斓
但不是我的终点
有一个遥远的地方
牵引着我的视线

或许走向遥远
依旧不是极限
我会再次出发
尽管脚步蹒跚

生命是一艘船
航行就是彼岸

1999 年

Words about Myself

If you taste a golden sweetness
Do not imagine the continuous emerald green
Corn is my commonplace name

If you experience a smooth flatness
Do not recall the once upright tree trunk
Bamboo mat is my cordial name

If you have a taste of sour-sweet
Do not miss the once immature beauty
Frozen pear is my pretty name.

January 23, 2020

自　述

如果尝到了那金色的微甜
真的不要想象　那曾经连片的翠绿
我有一个普通的名字　玉米

如果体验了那平坦的舒展
真的不要追忆　那曾经挺拔的身躯
我有一个亲切的名字　竹席

如果品过了那酸甜的滋味
真的不要怀念　那曾经青涩的美丽
我有一个俊俏的名字　冻梨

2020 年 1 月 23 日

Life

I admire this kind of life
Hold the aroma of a cup of tea in hand
Hold the warmth of a conversation in palms
Slumber in the games of others
Awake in my own deep intoxication

I yearn for this kind of life
Build an embankment due to a river's torrents
Feel moved due to a flower's blossom
Walk alone in the long empty avenue
Think quiet in the clamorous palace

I desire this kind of life
Wave a hand to bid farewell to darkness
Uphold a flag to summon up daybreak
Inspired only by dreams in heaven
Never vanquished by imagined difficulties

I seek this kind of life
Gather a flock of eagles to traverse the open sky
Be a grove of bamboos to break through the soil
Pave the roads I have already taken with fresh flowers
The roads I have chosen lead to perilous peaks.

January 21, 2020

人　生

欣赏这样的人生
握一杯茶的淡雅芬芳
捧一席话的殷殷温情
在别人的游戏里　酣睡
在自己的沉醉中　苏醒

向往这样的人生
因一条江的奔流筑堤
被一朵花的绽放感动
在无人的长街上　独行
在喧嚣的殿堂里　沉静

渴望这样的人生
挥一只手告别黑暗
举一面旗召唤黎明
只被空中的梦想　激励
不被想象的困难　战胜

追寻这样的人生
聚一群鹰凌空飞越
化一片竹破土而生
走过的路铺满了　鲜花
要走的路正通向　险峰

2020 年 1 月 21 日

You

The cloud is the most graceful thing in the world
Poets cannot take her away, or bid farewell to her
Much more graceful than the cloud is the wind
Singers sing her wholeheartedly, asking no questions

Even more graceful than the wind are you
Illusory as clouds, stirring as the wind
Like a ray of sunshine shining into the mundane
There is nothing before; there is all thriving after

Be wordless and speechless you
With a wind-like figure and a cloud-like look
It's enough to resemble in form, not in spirit
With serried mountain peaks behind, I ask not causation or harvest.

June 3, 2019

你

世界上最潇洒的 是 云
诗人们无法带走 挥手送行
比云更潇洒的 是 风
歌者们纵声吟唱 不问西东

比风更潇洒的 是 你
像云一样幻化 像风一样萌动
像一缕阳光照入平凡
此前一无所有 此后万物皆生

做一个无言无语的你
云一般的容颜 风一样的身影
貌似可也 何必神似
不问收获因果 身后叠嶂万重

2019 年 6 月 3 日

Voyage Home

A Salutation to All Fathers on Father's Day

The last spectacular dream
Is sailing home in dusk
Let each weather-beaten feather
Be soaked with golden sun rays

The last bit of pious hope
Is arriving ere the night home
Let each strand of dark-hued pursuit
Be left on the sea foams

The last stroke of all-out wielding
Is building a harbor in the hurricanes
Let each and every commonplace brick
Be infused with the comer's wind-braving strength

The last wisp of shining countenance
Is the eternal smile in the arms
Let the countless heroic take-offs in storm
Change into serenity after the wings are folded.

June 16, 2019

归航

——父亲节里致敬所有的父亲

最后一个 壮丽的梦想
是在暮色中 归航
让每一根 风雨淋湿的羽毛
都沾满 金色的阳光

最后一分 虔诚的愿望
是在夜色前 归航
让每一缕 暗黑色的追逐
都留在 身后的海面上

最后一下 全力的舞动
是在飓风中 建造海港
把每一块 普普通通的砖石
都注入 为来者抗风的力量

最后一缕 灿烂的表情
是在怀抱中 永恒微笑
那无数次 暴风雨中起飞的壮烈
全化为 这收羽后的无尽安详

2019 年 6 月 16 日

Who

Who is feeling sad, in lonely wandering
Who is feeling forlorn in the garden solitarily
Who is sobbing and whimpering in the vast darkness
Who is not seeing the sunlight even in days of brightness
Who has torn to pieces the letters, sprinkling them on the grass
Who, after shaking off the chains, still feels disconsolate
Who, after yearning, has stopped yearning
Who, after crossing the limit of hope, is walking toward despair
—Who regards himself
As a boat overturned on the sea of life

Who is rising toward the moon, repeatedly, like the fearless sea
Who is calling the stars, affectionately, like the towering mountains
Who is holding the earth tightly, though weak as the short grass
Who is seeking homeland restlessly, as the wind stirs the fountains
Who is thinking of opening the gate to let the spring in
Who is going to extend his hands among the giant rocks
Who is marching on again, after being stricken to the ground
Who is still hoping, after falling into despair
—Who trusts himself
To be able to light up the sun, even against the attack of storm.

Draft on December 10, 1986

是 谁

是谁在孤独的徘徊中暗自忧伤
是谁在寂寞的花园里独自彷徨
是谁在无边的黑暗中低声抽泣
是谁在晴朗的日子里也看不到阳光
是谁撕碎了一页页信笺在草地上挥撒
是谁挣开了锁链却又无比惆怅
是谁在憧憬之后已不再憧憬
是谁越过了希望的极限走向了绝望
——是谁认定自己
已经覆舟 在人生的海洋

是谁像无畏的大海一次次扑向月亮
是谁像高耸的山峦深情地呼唤星光
是谁像低矮的小草却紧紧地拥抱大地
是谁像永不疲倦的风儿不停地寻找自己的故乡
是谁想打开大门让春天驰进
是谁想在巨大的山岩中伸出双掌
是谁在跌倒之后还在前行
是谁在失望之后还在希望
——是谁相信自己
能在暴风雨中 点亮太阳

1986年12月10日草

Afraid

Since you've chosen to go afar, you should not fear snow or frost
Since you've had it once, how can you not see it pass
Then there will be nothing that you cannot bear
Then there will be nothing that you cannot imagine
Shrink and eke out a miserable life; a large body will feel half dead
Die into rebirth; a thin and weak figure will emit resplendent rays

The only fear is winning success yet neglecting sharing
The other fear is experiencing tribulation yet reaping no growth
I am also afraid of frittering away the time yet the scenery missing
Looking back and finding behind you complete desolation
The biggest fear is winning applauses yet losing directions
Having true love, the sealed heart rejects openness

Do not blame greed
A small transcendence is a rebirth
Do not curse fear
Learning to fear is a real growth
Forget Self; embrace a natural grace all with your life
Practice No-Self; approach incessantly happy liberation.

First draft on June 15, 2019

Revised on March 29, 2020

怕

既然选择远行 不要怕雨雪风霜
既然曾经拥有 怎能不承受消亡
那就 没有什么 不能担当
那就 没有什么 难以想象
畏缩苟延 庞大的躯体也是半僵
向死而生 羸弱者映出灿烂的光芒

怕只怕 赢得了成功 忽略了分享
经历了磨难 没收获成长
还害怕 蹉跎光阴 错失一路风光
蓦然回首 身后满是荒凉
最害怕 获得了掌声 失去了方向
拥有了真情 封闭的心灵没有开放

别责备贪婪
超越一点点 就是一次新生
不怪罪恐惧
学会了害怕 才是真正的生长
忘我 用一生去拥抱 这轻盈的飘逸
无我 每一天无限趋近 那幸福的解放

2019 年 6 月 15 日初稿

2020 年 3 月 29 日修订

Remonstration and Self-remonstration

I

The game is still going on
Having only passed half-time
The Forward and Rear running
Forget why they strive

II

The pen in hand
Is a sword of mind
Occasionally for fighting used
In most cases, for self-reflection

III

You have seen clearly
Each word I wrote on paper
Yet cannot get the meaning
Not our common embarrassment

IV

Take care to tidy up the mood
Line up your strength in a parade
Build your last line of defense
Halt all retreats, and prepare to assault.

Beginning of Spring, February 3, 2021

谏与自谏

（一）

比赛远未结束
只是刚过了中场
奔跑的 前锋后卫
忘记了为什么拼抢

（二）

掌心的笔
是思想的刀
偶尔用于搏杀
主要用来自剖

（三）

你看清了
纸上的每一个字
却读不懂 我说的话
这不是我们 共同的尴尬

（四）

注意调整心情
把力量 排成队形
筑起最后的防线
停止一切退却 准备发起冲锋

2021 年 2 月 3 日 立春之日

No Fortification in My Heart

No calling, no echoing
March birches are quietly listening
At the horizon the fiery-red sunset glow
Is burning the serene dusk's halo

No fortification there is in my heart
The gate of the castle is to all open
Ten thousand guesses you may bring
And walk into my open bosom

Do not bring your long sword, for fear of the dark night
You should close your cautionary eyes
There will be yet another way
For you to see people's countenance gay

Do not worry about the long distance ahead
You need only to climb a muddy mountain
No fortification there is in my heart
Nor is there a thick layer of unmelted ice.

March 5, 1987

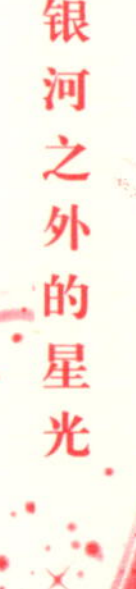

我的心灵没有设防

没有呼唤 也没有回声
三月的白桦树在静静地倾听
天边火红的晚霞
燃烧着黄昏的寂静

我的心灵没有设防
城堡的大门向所有的人敞开
你可以带上一万种猜想
走进我坦荡的胸怀

不要因为惧怕黑夜而带上你的长剑
你要闭上戒备的眼睛
将会有另一种方式
让你看清人们的面容

不要担心路途遥远
只是要翻越一道泥泞的山岭
我的心灵没有设防
也没有未化的冰层

1987 年 3 月 5 日

State of Being

In my heart there is awe
In my eyes there is rival
Walk and have a road ahead
Lie down and have time and space

Care not if I win or lose
Care only the feelings of the ones I care
Calculate not the rewards for your efforts
Calculate the seemingly irrelevant tidings and worries

If you are my beloved
I care not if you are rich, poor, pretty or ugly
If I do not love you
I care not if you are in the limelight or at the crest of charm.

10 pm, May 23, 2020

状 态

心中有敬畏
眼中有对手
走着的时候有道路
躺下的片段有宇 和宙

不在乎自己的输赢
只在乎 自己在乎的人的感受
不计较付出后的回报
关心着 那似乎不相干的喜报和烦忧

若爱的是你
就不想你的贫富美丑
若不在乎你
哪管你风头正劲 万众风流

2020 年 5 月 23 日晚 10 时

Myself[1]

Looking at my graying hair gradually thicken
Seeing the wrinkles quicken in corners of my eyes
I accept my awful table manners at an elegant dinner
I cannot help my quick tempers at a difficult moment
My Dear, all this is nothing
Everyone should be true to himself

Try hard to restrain foolish greed
Unrestrained is fear for the unknown
Care not people's show of felicity
Yet grudge success in vicinity
My Dear, all this is nothing
Everyone has a concealed true self

① At 18, I read the famous French writer Romain Rolland's *Jean Christophe*. Now, its plot is totally forgotten, only the poem in its Preface is venerated as motto, and becomes a lifelong memory: Ten years of bitter struggle is against myself, without taking oneself as enemy, how can we triumph ?
Having fought with myself for half the life / Enlightenment comes during deep meditation / Accepting and admiring oneself Is the higher aim of life / And an award conferred on one who fights with oneself / This is also a premise for one to accept and appreciate others' selves / Loving the myriads of other selves is the greater love.

自 己[①]

眼看着鬓间 白发渐渐浓密
欣赏着眼角 皱纹细碎隆起
在雅致的席间 接受了自己的吃相
在艰难的时刻 没忍住自己的脾气
亲 这一切 都没有什么
每个人 都是一个真实的自己

努力克制 那愚蠢的贪婪
压抑不住 对未知的恐惧
看到秀出的幸福 不屑
面对周围的成功 妒忌
亲 这一切 也没有什么
每个人 都有一个隐秘的自己

---

① 18 岁，读法国著名作家罗曼·罗兰的《约翰·克利斯朵夫》。如今，情节全已忘记，唯卷首诗被奉为人生座右铭而铭记终生：“十年的苦斗，对抗着自己，不把自己当成敌人，我们怎能胜利？”
在与自己搏斗半生之后 / 在深思中再悟 / 接受和欣赏自己 / 才是更高的境界 / 是对与自己苦斗的自己的自我奖励 / 也是接受和欣赏他人的自己的前提 / 热爱亿万个不同的自己 / 就是大爱的终极

It is said that humans of all beings suffer the most
Eventually, a transcendental life gives most gratification
A hundred years of bitter struggle is against oneself
Thirty thousand days and nights witness my admiring
In my dream at night, Romain Rolland revises his tenet—
Never be an enemy unto thy own self
I embrace victory together with myself.

July 7, 2019

都说是 世间万苦人最苦

到头来 超越的人生最惬意

百年的苦斗 对抗着自己

三万个日夜 欣赏着自己

夜梦罗曼·罗兰 修订罗氏定律

不以自己为敌

我 和自己一起胜利

2019 年 7 月 7 日

Pray

I pray tomorrow the sun also rises
A new night in time will bloom
I pray after withering, the flower again opens
The next blossoming is your smiling face
My prayers are in such repetitions, simple and direct
They traverse long distances and turnings
Until eventually is the answer revealed
And this is already my highest wish.

I pray tomorrow the sun also rises
A new night in time will bloom
I pray after withering, the flower again opens
The next blossoming is your smiling face
My prayers are in such repetitions, simple and direct
They traverse long distances and turnings
Until eventually is the answer revealed
And this is already my highest wish.

August 9, 2020

祈　祷

我祈祷 明天太阳照样升起
新的黑夜如期而绽
我祈祷 花谢之后仍有花开
下一个面孔 是你的笑颜
我的祈祷如此重复 直接而简单
要走过很多里程 和回转
才能 揭晓答案
这已经是最高的祝愿

我祈祷 明天太阳照样升起
新的黑夜如期而绽
我祈祷 花谢之后仍有花开
下一个面孔 是你的笑颜
我的祈祷如此重复 直接而简单
要走过很多里程 和回转
才能 揭晓答案
这已经是最高的祝愿

2020 年 8 月 9 日

Esteem

Esteem a vine's efforts to climb
Twining the boulder on the left, on the right the grits pushing
Esteem a water drop's wish to rise
Leaving no stains or traces, no fogs or rosy clouds floating

Esteem a cat's pursuit
From the wall to the tree, from the chair to the bed
Esteem a dog's happy being
In smelling, chasing, barking and laughing

Esteem a broken cord, praising its past connection
Esteem a streamer ray, saluting its brilliant moment
Esteem an autumn fruit, giving spring a formal closure
Esteem a trace of winter, returning the field a full summer

Esteem a grain of dust, like looking up to the whole universe
Esteem a footprint, more than all the bustling luxuriance
Esteem a warm teardrop, like embracing endless lakes and rivers
Esteem a farewell, like restarting the secret codes of nirvanas.

December 12, 2020

尊　重

尊重一棵藤的攀爬
左绕巨石　右顶粗砂
尊重一滴水的升腾
无渍无痕　无雾无霞

尊重一只猫的求索
从墙到树　从椅到榻
尊重一条狗的快乐
时嗅时逐　时吼时哈

尊重一根断线　赞美曾经的连接
尊重一束射光　致敬闪烁的刹那
尊重一枚秋果　给春天一个结局
尊重一片冬迹　还田野一个盛夏

尊重一粒尘埃　就像敬望整个宇宙
尊重一个脚印　胜过赞美所有的繁华
尊重一滴热泪　好似拥抱无尽的江河
尊重一场告别　仿佛重启涅槃的密码

2020 年 12 月 12 日

A Flash of Memory on the Street

My Primary School Teacher Touched Me on the Forehead

Wind blows over the high sky
Fish swims across the deep sea
That afternoon when sunlight warmed the eye
All of a sudden, my mind's eye did see
A hand where tenderness and warmth lie
That had caressed this very forehead of me

At this very moment several decades later
Days and nights by the thousand flowing away
My heart is woken up by a memory
Established in life, by no doubts led astray
Amid the busy traffic, I am standing, a spectator
My cheeks were bathed in tears, my laughers were gay

The rain was flowing by the corner of the street
My tears were flowing through the corner of my eyes
That hand radiating with warmth and heat
Traveled through time to the Beijing streets with surprise
To feel, once more, my one-time childlike heart beat
Flicking away dust and wrapping it in a new disguise.

January 26, 2021

街头突忆

——被小学老师抚摸额头

风 从高空飞过
鱼 在深海游过
阳光灿烂的那个下午
突然 记起
一只温暖的手
曾在这个额头 抚过

几十年后的 这个时刻
白天和黑夜 流走了 上万个
这被记忆唤醒的心灵
而立 又不惑
站在车水马龙间
泪流满面地笑着

雨 在街角淌过
泪 在眼角流过
那只温暖的手
穿越到了 北京街头
把曾经的童心 再次抚摸
拂去轻尘 重新包裹

2021 年 1 月 26 日

Freedom

Many and many a year ago
I admired birds, pretty or ugly
For freely they could migrate
I admire evening winds, gentle or strong
For freely they could breathe
A thriving seed I was
Shouldering boulders' weight
A so-called screw I was
Fixed to the spot by a merciless giant thumb

Desiring freedom
I walk from space to space
Seeking freedom
I walk through fogs and suffer love's tides
Places more spacious obtained
Which yet turned into bigger cages, firm and erect
I have a soul of freedom
Yet not a body freestanding

自　由

很多年以前
我羡慕美丽或丑陋的鸟儿
能够自由地迁徙
羡慕急骤或柔和的晚风
能够自由地呼吸
我是颗蓬勃的种子
承受着巨石的压抑
我是颗所谓的螺丝钉
被一只无情的巨手　按在了原地

渴望自由
从一片天地　走向另一片天地
追寻自由
穿越世俗的迷雾　也承受情感的潮汐
收获了一个个更大的空间
却演化成更大的囚笼　牢牢伫立
我有自由的灵魂
却没有自由的身躯

Darkling, I try to perceive heaven and earth
Experiencing Lao Zi's heaven-man oneness
Perhaps, the true freedom of all worth
Is everybody's right in seeking freedom
Perhaps, the true freedom
Is always at the bottom of our heart.

June, 1998

冥冥中 我感悟天地

体味老子的天人合一

或许 真正的自由

是我们人人拥有的 追求自由的权利

或许 真正的自由

一直就停留在 我们的心底

1998 年 6 月

Simplicity

I quietly listened to your song
Thus I was loved by you once
I gently read your words
Thus I have loved you once

You rolled your eyes at me
I returned with a smiling face
This world of beauty
Is as simple as such.

February 9, 2021

简　单

静静地 听你的歌
就这样 被你爱了一次
悄悄地 读你的字
就这样 淡淡地 爱你一次

你翻我 一个白眼
我回你 一个笑脸
这个美丽世界
就是这么简单

2021 年 2 月 9 日

Proving

With all sorts of methods, I try to prove
Living is like budding or smiling
Like making sounds or breathing sometimes
Even, like a gaze or a heart beat

With all sorts of ways, I try to prove
Having lived is like in writing or thinking
Like painting or carving sometimes
Even, like a scratch or burning.

January 24, 2021

证　明

用各种方法 证明

活着 比如萌动 比如微笑

有时是呼吸 或声音

甚至 凝视 和心跳

用各种方式 证明

活过 比如书写 比如思考

有时是涂抹 或刻印

甚至 划痕 和燃烧

2021 年 1 月 24 日

Temper

Light-Heartedly Dedicated to You, Him, Me and Hahaha

【 I 】Let me tell you, and you all
I am a man with a temper
No one dares to bully me
My pride cannot be challenged

【 You 】Dear, Dearest Dears
In the streets there is no lack of quick-tempered men
To see who is quicker-tempered, you need to line up now
I know their number must exceed 100 in a row

【 (S)He 】Dear, Dearest Ones
Rarer than pandas are those who have no temper
Lose temper to yourself, for the last time
Then go tamely to bed, and wake up blending with light or dust

【 Passer-by 】My Dears, My Dearest Ones
I too want to be a man with fierce tempers
Like a bulging balloon, I wait to be played
I adore beating, be the end rapture or fracture.

July 29, 2019

脾　气

——戏赠我你他 以及哈哈哈

【我】 告诉你 还有你们
我是一个 有脾气的人
没有人能够 欺负我
最不能挑战的 是我的傲娇自尊

【你】亲啊亲 亲爱的亲
马路上最不缺 有脾气的人
要比脾大还是气大 赶紧去排队吧
我认识的脾气王 肯定超过一百人

【TA】亲爱的亲 亲爱的们
比大熊猫更少的 是没脾气的人
对自己的脾气 发最后一顿脾气吧
然后乖乖睡觉 醒来后和光同尘

【路人甲】我的亲啊 我的们
我也想做 一个有脾气的人
像一个鼓鼓的气球 等人拍
重拍之后 哪管销魂 还是惊魂

2019 年 7 月 29 日

The Change

Won the debate; but lost the balance
Won small gains; lost the respect
Won the battle; lost the war
Won the years; lost the life

Give up stubbornness, and gain true love
Give up vanity, and gain respect
Give up inertia, and gain a prospect new
Give up plain lands, and gain the heights

The change does appear in an instant
Turn, and you witness a thousand scenes.

February 2, 2021

变 局

赢得了辩论 失去了平衡
赢得了小利 失去了尊重
赢得了战役 失去了战争
赢得了岁月 失去了人生

放下了倔强 收获了真情
放下了颜面 收获了致敬
放下了惯性 收获了新程
放下了平坦 收获了高峰

变局 就在 一念之间
转身 笑拥 万千风景

2021 年 2 月 2 日

The Night Banquet

Master Li Bai planned
A night banquet for himself
Inviting the bright moon and the clear shadow
Not knowing how many jars of wine we needed
How many chopsticks, how many glasses and plates

A dinner with wine, for one man
Can be turned into a grand banquet
For ten thousand guests; drinking alone without wine
Drinking clear water only, sparkling eyes
Can be turned into drunken eyes, swelling with tears

Li Bai's dinner party has lasted a thousand years
The heroes willing to be drunk changed each night
The accompanying bright moon, as wished, comes in sight
Only the wordless shadow clear and bright
Proves a loyal partner under a bit of candle light.

January 31, 2021

夜 宴

李白老师 策划了
一个人的夜宴
邀了明月 又请了清影
只是不知 有几瓮残酒
几双竹筷 几副杯盘

有酒之席 一个人的
饭局 能吃成一万人的
盛宴 无酒独酌
清水小饮 闪亮的明眸
喝成 热泪盈眶的 醉眼

李白的饭局 千年未散
求醉的主角 每晚更换
作陪的明月 随心出现
只有沉默的清影
凭一点烛光 忠诚相伴

2021 年 1 月 31 日

【Episode Four】
The Horizon Always Following Behind

【第四季】
身后总有地平线

The Moment of Humility

After Reading the Tao Te Ching, I

Riding a green bull, unhurriedly, you left Hangu Pass
This leaving is to last thousand years

Only the water, gentle and yielding
Amid the land, the sky and the ocean
In endless cycles is still running
Only the water, sharp and pointing
In soils, rocks and bodies of plants and animals
Time's extension line is still carving
Only the water, modest and humble
Towards the lowest places is still pouring or flowing
Yet all life's spaces it fills

The earthen road you walked on is still there
Now called rail, now called air routes
The wheels you marveled at are still running
Crushing mileages of desire
Leaving behind unfulfilled dreams
Many stories are going round
No matter what the legends
Their content stays eternally unchanged
Many lives are handed down
Literati still sing of love; archeologists still eulogize procreation.

March 1, 2001

谦卑之刻

——读《道德经》有感之一

骑一头青牛 你幽幽地出了函谷关
这一走 就是几千年

只有柔弱的水啊
依旧在陆地 天空和海洋之间
无休止地循环
只有锋利的水啊
依旧在土壤 岩石和动植物的躯干
雕刻着时光的延长线
只有谦卑的水啊
依旧向低洼处倾泻或流淌
却充盈着所有生命的空间

你走过的那条土路 依旧在顺延
有时叫轨道 有时叫航线
你感叹的那些车轮 依旧在旋转
碾过的 是欲望的里程
抛下的 是未了的心愿
有许多故事在流传
无论传说怎样改变
传说中的东西亘古不变
有许多生命在流传
文人们赞美爱情 考古者称颂繁衍

2001年3月1日

The Illusion of Time

After Reading the Tao Te Ching, II

You are changing; Heaven does not
Heaven is changing; Tao does not
Tao is changing; you do not
It is impossible to live eternally in the river of thought
Better to meditate on the coast of the sea of reality
For many like Yinxi① whom life has brought to this world
They have to face up to inescapable spatiality
—Desires are still driven by the body
Pains are still suffered by the heart

Wherever you go, you walk in time
Wherever you stand, the horizon is behind
Wherever you live, you can never shun the confusion of blessings or disasters
Wherever you die, you can never find the illusory refuge of being and non-being.

March 1, 2001

① Yinxi is a legendary figure of Zhou Dynasty, a guard at the western gate of the Zhou capital, who importuned the sage Lao Zi to compose the Tao Te Ching before permitting him to pass.

时光之幻

——读《道德经》有感之二

你在改变 天不变
天在改变 道不变
道在改变 你不变
不能 永生在思想的河流里
不妨 沉思在现实的大海边
生活中 很多无奈的尹喜
面对的是 无法逃遁的空间
——欲望仍由肉体驱使
痛苦仍由心灵承担

走在哪里 都是走在时光里
站在哪里 身后总有地平线
生在哪里 也躲不开福与祸的迷惘
死在哪里 也离不了有与无的变幻

2001 年 3 月 1 日

He Who Knows Does Not Speak

After Reading the Tao Te Ching, III

Better to remain silent
And see the silence of heaven, earth and the myriads of things
Better to remain still
And appreciate the unchanging Tao, name and origin of all things
Better to remain forbearing
And act with no intention, with non-action, recompense injury
with blessings
Better to remain restrained
First, gentleness; second economy; and third no precedence
over others
I see; I know; I understand
Yet he who knows does not speak

Your meeting with Confucius
Must have been a conversation between the wise
Wonder if you have circled the borderline between action
and non-action
Or drawn the demarcation line between benevolence
and non-benevolence
You saw; you thought; you talked
But you took no action
Leaving only some laughers gay:
For governing a country is like stewing river shrimps or sea fish.

March 1, 2001

知者不言

——读《道德经》有感之三

不如沉默吧
看天无言 地无言 万物无言
不如静止吧
品不变的道 不变的名 不变的万物本源
不如隐忍吧
为无为 事无事 以德报怨
不如退让吧
一曰慈 二曰俭 三曰不敢为天下先
我明了 我晓得 我理解
但是知者不言

你和孔子的见面
一定是智者间的交谈
不知是否圈定了 为与不为的临界点
不知是否划清了 仁与不仁的分界线
你看了 你想了 你说了
却什么也没做
只留几声呵呵地笑
治理大国好像清炖 几条河虾海鲜

2001 年 3 月 1 日

’Tis Also Life

Having weighed it on my mind, and taken the High Speed Rail
Having had a glass of wine, and made several gossips
Having crossed many bridges and roads and found
them not different
I find the grapes not eaten are not as sour as you imagine

Having bent and straightened the back, one is
refreshed immensely
Having had instants of falling down, I want to lie there longer
At the youthful age of thirty, I want to brandish the tiger fork
At the prime age of fifty, I had my waist sprained in the attempt

It is only many years later that I start to think of a word of gratitude
When I’m able to repay kindness, time has my
benefactors dispersed
At the age of seventy, let me forgo my creditor’s rights to reclaim
At the age of ninety, my greatest wish is to hear Mum calling
me home

I came, I passed, I took it up, and I put it down
The last chance of forgiveness is reserved for yourself
Whenever you meet, do utter a heart-felt farewell
And regard the next reunion as the first meeting
after reincarnation.

November 28, 2019

也是生活

想了一会儿心事 搭了一班高铁
喝上几杯小酒 唠叨几段实话
走过了那么多桥 和路没什么两样
没有吃到的葡萄们 其实不是酸的啊

弯腰后再直起 那叫个意气风发
那些跌倒的片刻 真想多躺一阵子
三十岁的年华 想舞一舞钢叉
五十岁的光阴 小腰闪了一下下

总是多年之后 才想到说声谢谢啊
能够报恩的时节 恩人们被岁月带远了
七十岁的人生 把难收的债权弃了吧
九十岁的愿望 想听妈妈喊我回家

来过了 路过了 拿起了 放下了
最后的原谅 一定要留给自己啊
在每一个相聚的日子 好好告个别吧
将下一次重逢 当作轮回后的初见刹那

2019 年 11 月 28 日

'Tis Still Life

Mohe City's summer holiday is a so-called summer holiday
Sansha City's winter holiday is a so-called winter holiday
The love-laden West Lake is at times cloud-laden
And surging through congestion, instantly becomes Three Gorges

Several lone peaks' eternal silence of
A section of the river's flowing elegance
With saints and sages, I look up to the starry skies
Facing the tree hole, my eloquence fails

Abandoning the subtle mysteries worshipped by all
Forgetting the connection code in used-by period
Donning blue jeans, I quietly appraise red wine's acidic taste
Pursing lips to hide eye wrinkles, I clench my teeth with a smile.

November 11, 2020

还是生活

漠河的暑假　也叫暑假
三沙的寒假　还是寒假
多情的西湖　也许未晴
奔腾冲破了拥堵　顿成三峡

几座孤峰的永恒沉默
一段江流的潇潇洒洒
和圣贤一起　仰望了星空
独对树洞　却说不出话

放下了众生膜拜的缥缈奥秘
遗忘了有效期内的联接密码
套上蓝色牛仔　静品红酒的酸涩
抿嘴藏好眼皱　含笑扣紧双牙

2020 年 11 月 11 日

Winter Solstice · 2020

Heavy snow is coming, no fireplace to sit around
I wait for Boreas to blow my wishes to the snow country
Heavy snow is coming, yet I cannot bear to sleep,
struggling to keep eyes open
Afraid of being lost in haziness, more afraid of missing the
spotlessly white

The day is fading out, its shimmer sinking into the twilight
Cold accident and iron will have entered a fierce fight
The day is fading, the dark closing in on the deer herd
Unfettered winter birds dart forward, making their wild songs

Heavy snow comes quietly, the dusk stands lonesome
In boundless light and shade, flakes of my thoughts are
desolately falling
Waiting for the serene moment when wind dies and trees
cease hustling
I build a small, cozy nest and hide a vast flowing glacier.

December 21, 2020

冬　至 · 2020

大雪即来 没有围坐的炉火
等待着朔风 把心愿吹向雪国
大雪即来 努力睁眼 不忍入眠
怕在朦胧中失落 更怕把洁白错过

白昼将逝 微光坠入了暮色
冰冷的意外 开始 和钢铁的意志相搏
白昼将逝 暗夜合围着群鹿
无羁的冬雀 疾飞 开启了野性的狂歌

大雪无声而来 黄昏满身落寞
漫天的光影下 思想的雪粒 萧然飞落
等待 风停树静的 沉谧片刻
筑一个温热的小巢 藏一条浩瀚的冰河

2020 年 12 月 21 日

Winter Solstice · 2019

Winter Solstice has arrived; Minor Cold is impending
Boundless dark clouds lock the low smog
Thinking of the thousand-mile rivers frozen with ice
I care more about vegetables and rice

The last few fallen leaves with tree trunks have parted
Returning to dust at building corners and roadsides
Zhichun Road Subway is crossing subterranean
Gusts of the north wind are courting the spring tides

How I crave from the sky snow drifting and falling
I love the icy cold days! Isn't that chill thrilling?
Roll up the worry of my mind into a snowball shining
In my burning heart veins, the sealed wish is crystallizing.

February 30, 2019

冬　至·2019

冬至已至　小寒即来
无边的阴云　锁住低垂的雾霾
想念着　千里冰封下的江河
然后　再关心一下粮食和蔬菜

最后几片落叶　早已告别树干
在楼角和路边　回归尘埃
知春路的地下铁　在底层穿行
阵阵北风呼啸着　向春天告白

期盼着一场　漫天的雪啊
喜欢冰天寒彻　冻得不亦快哉
把一捧心事　攥入雪球
那封印的愿望　就结晶在火热的心脉

2019 年 12 月 30 日

Carriage

Some people stand; others kneel
Some kneeling people stand
Others standing kneel
You worship your primordial gods
I love my vast fertile land

Some think the people standing are kneeling
Some think themselves kneeling are standing
Some feel standing makes them nobler
Some believe the so-called kneeling has more meaning
You exhibit your handsomeness; I seek my fearlessness

Some see their standing selves standing
Some perceive their kneeling selves standing
Some kneel to history, standing; some stand at the end, kneeling
You chase height, applause, and splendor
I desire hot blood, frozen land and tracelessly disappearing

This is my one and only choice
Prostrating on the deeply-loved land
This is my life's destiny: becoming spring mud by all trodden
This is the all-despising immortality, the eternity beyond sight
No standing, no kneeling, no entreating, for the last drop to burn out.

10 pm, July 26, 2020

姿

有的人站着 有的人跪着
有些站着的人 跪着
有些跪着的人 站着
你敬你的 万古神祇
我爱我的 苍茫大地

有些人以为 站着的别人 跪着
有些人认为 跪着的自己 站着
有些人觉得 站立更显高贵
有些人坚信 所谓的跪姿 才是意义
你显你的潇洒 我求我的无惧

有些人看见 站立着的自己 站着
有些人透见 跪着的自己 站着
有些站者跪向了历史 有些跪者站在了终极
你追逐挺拔 喝彩 和绚烂
我渴望热血融入 广袤的冰原 消失无迹

这是我选择的唯一
匍匐在深爱的土地
这是我一生的归宿 化为任人践踏的春泥
这是傲视一切的不朽 那看不见的永恒
无站无立 无跪无祈 只因燃尽了 最后一滴

2020年7月26日晚10时

Aspect

When I hold out my hands
I am not craving satisfaction above my expectation
I just want to grasp gently
The airy fragrance bestowed by Mother Earth to her creation

When I hold my palms together
I am not praying for help from the void
I just want to recast
The unsettled mind in my bosom into non-action

When I lower my head
I am not giving up to gullies and stony obstruction
I just want to pick up faster
The happiness lost in the dust

When I bend over
I am not giving in to it, or them, in desperation
I just want to arch my back, more steadily uphold
Your jumping feet, my most beloved, in devotion.

January 15, 2021

态

当我 伸出手的时候
不是奢求 那超出期待的 满足
只是要 把大地恩赐的
芬芳 在空中 轻轻握住

当我 合上掌的时候
不是祈祷 那来自虚无的 帮助
只是要 把动荡不安的
寸心 在胸口 重新浇铸

当我 低下头的时候
不是向顽石 还有沟壑 认输
只是要 更快地 拾起
那失落在 尘埃中的 幸福

当我 弯下腰的时候
不是向它 还有它们 屈服
只是要 拱背 更稳地托起
最爱的你 起跳的 双足

2021 年 1 月 15 日

Degree

Warmth has degrees
The low means coolness
The high boiling hotness

Adamancy has hardness
The soft is frailness
The hard desolate loneliness

The River of Life has depth
The shallow is still flowing
The deep vast immensity

An innocent heart knows no limit
Its emptiness is spotless
Its brimming is colorful.

February 24, 2020

度

温暖 是有刻度的
低了 是凉爽
高了 是滚烫

坚强 是有硬度的
柔了 是软弱
刚了 是落寞

生命的河 是有深度的
浅处 是静流
深处 是浩瀚

赤子的心 没有限度
空旷 一尘不染
充盈 万物斑斓

2020 年 2 月 24 日

No Title · 2019

It is better to take a subway train
Each and every face
Is before your eyes, clear and plain
Whoever steps on another's foot will say
I'm sorry
Then behold the eight teeth in a smiling face

In times of luck, one will see
An enlivened face
Whose story in boredom I supplement my brain with
Passing the Auto-gate, with unnatural grace
I snap my cellphone to the automatic payee
And walking in haste, I forget many a face
That I have just passed, being busy as a bee.

March 1, 2019

无　题·2019

还是乘地铁比较好
每一张脸
都在眼前　真真切切
不管被谁踩了脚　都说一声
对不起
然后　看见八颗牙齿在微笑

幸运的时候　会看到
一张生动的脸
无聊地　脑补他或她的故事
出闸机　故作潇洒地
扣上手机支付
匆匆地前行　忘记了
刚刚错过了那么多的人

2019 年 3 月 1 日

No Title · 2018

Ere the Mid-autumn moon rises
The sunshine of Yonghe Lamasery is oscillating
Not so much due to the autumn's bleak scenes
As to the laziness of my own mind

At the alley entrance are backpackers in twos or threes
The chairs of the coffee shop are utterly empty
High is the blue sky, and far are the white clouds
True and tangible are the long, red walls only.

September 24, 2018

无　题·2018

在中秋的月亮升起之前
雍和宫的阳光在摇摇晃晃
算不上所谓的秋意萧索
只是有一点懒洋洋

胡同口的背包客三三两两
咖啡店的群椅空空荡荡
蓝天高了　白云远了
真真切切的　是眼前的长长红墙

2018 年 9 月 24 日

Drunk

I must've been drunk, because
I remember my gender and my attire today
I remember my mum, dad, and dear dears
I remember, too, I should not borrow too much money

Definitely, definitely drunk
I remember those I care about and feel reluctant to part
I remember my nationality and hometown
I remember, too, in this life I have made efforts and exertions

Alright, good, alright. A bit drunk.
I remember I made many efforts and had few regrets
The regrets I remember, however, I can do nothing about
Drunk not dead, I'm reassured and fall asleep.

8 pm, Start of Spring, February 3, 2021

醉

肯定 是多了
记得 自己的性别 今天的衣着
记得 妈妈 爸爸 亲 亲们
还记得 钱 应该不欠太多

绝对 绝对 是多了
记得 自己在乎的那些不舍
记得 国籍 和故乡
还记得 这一生 好像努力过

好吧 好的 好吧 好的 有点儿醉了
记得努力的不少 记得遗憾不多
记得的遗憾 却又无可奈何
醉了 又不是死了 干脆睡吧

2021年2月3日 立春之日晚8时

Tipsy

Sip a goblet of red wine from South America
As if having kissed the sunlight of the Southern hemisphere
Open a few bottles of aged alcohol from Chishui River
I no longer will desire European wineries

Saluting my soul
My eased fingers compose a few lines of passing thoughts
Aiming at the vast emptiness
My thought pulls the trigger, shooting this glass of boldness.

February 15, 2021

醺

品 一杯南美的红酒
吻了 南半球的阳光
开几瓶 赤水河的陈酿
不再向往 欧罗巴的酒庄

向灵魂致意
舒展的手指 写几句随想
向虚空瞄准
思维扣动扳机 发射这樽张扬

2021 年 2 月 15 日

Land · 1984

Mountain-torrents cleave open your skin
Intersected blood vessels are exposed in your chest
A thousand joint protrusions are seen on the back of your hand
The yellow blood often rush downward, swirling up the rocks
The stubborn grass trembles in the northwest wind
The mountain eagle circles the silent mountain top
Villages sparse as stars lean against a few lonely old willows
(As if never able to exit the forest-like hills
O the lonesome loess roads, endless and non-stop)

Make their new skin golden, golden like your corns
Make their golden skin rough, rough like yourself, O land
Make their rough skin dry and cracked; kiss your hot dry air
Often do the fierce gales spray the golden gravel and sand
To each of their pores
Men and women of the land the most solemn baptism
have received
Precipitating too many tribulations, the rivers flow, carrying
immortal hopes
People on both sides are waiting for a long, long time
For the sunrises described a thousand times in the cycle of myths
(Finally, now, the autumn sorghums have dotted the hills
with red gifts)

土　地·1984

山洪切开了你的皮肤
交错的血管裸露在你的胸口
千万个粗大的骨节凸起在你的手背
常常有黄色的血液　席卷着山石奔流
倔强的小草在西北风中战栗
山鹰旋绕在沉默的山头
星星般疏落的村庄　背倚着几株苍凉的老柳
（仿佛永远也走不出这森林般的丘陵
寂寞的黄土路啊　悠悠　悠悠）

使他们新生的皮肤金黄　金黄得像你的玉米
使他们金黄的皮肤粗糙　粗糙得像你啊　土地
使他们粗糙的皮肤干裂　亲吻你炎燥的空气
常常有狂风　把金黄的沙砾
撒向他们的每一个毛孔
土地上的男人女人们　经受了　最庄严的洗礼
沉淀了太多的苦难　江河流动着不朽的希望
两岸的人们在久久地等待
等待那轮神话中　描述过千万次的朝阳
（终于　这一刻　秋天的高粱点红了山岗）

Today, you are clearer and brighter than ever
Today, you are more brilliant and shining than ever
'Tis not because of wind and sand, not because of wind and sand
That turned my singing hoarse, hoarse, and blurred my eyes
(My universe is budding with reveries of you and the spring after).

November 14, 1984

今天 你比任何时候都清晰 明亮

今天 你比任何时候都灿烂 辉煌

不是由于风沙不是由于风沙

沙哑了沙哑了我的歌唱 模糊了模糊了我的目光

（我的宇宙中萌动着 关于你和春天以后的遐想）

1984 年 11 月 14 日

Land · 2010

I gaze at the snow-capped mountains, I see uninhibited wind whizz and whirl
Engage the glacier in talk, I find the frozen water wordless for a thousand years
Canyons and ravines, shallow or deep
Are the latitude and longitude lines carved by flowing waters
Dwarf rocks and perilous peaks arranged at random
Are the weather-beaten to pieces of time
The silent lake supports its edge with hard firmness
The restless village has fallen into a victim of the city's expansion

Bid farewell to the divine, I judge in the name of the days to come
Pick chrysanthemums and row a boat, I compose a graceful new chapter
The boundless past by the wind is blown away
Fading into the expanse of the clear blue space overhead
Waving my hand, I bid a decisive farewell to suffering
The steps are so heavy, and the calling so distant
Standing on a small bridge over a flowing stream, seeing the solitary desert smoke rising
The new dreamy reincarnation is hidden between the lines of the history scrolls

土　地·2010

凝望这片雪山　不羁的风呼啸飞旋
对话这块冰川　凝固的水万载无言
深浅不一的峡谷沟壑
是流水雕刻的经纬线
高低错落的险峰矮岩
是风化成碎片的时间
静寂的湖泊　艰难地支撑着自己的边缘
躁动的村庄　失陷于都市的不断蔓延

告别神灵　以未来的名义进行审判
泛舟采菊　用诗人的优雅挥就新篇
无边往事被风吹散
消失在那片清澈的蔚蓝
挥一挥手　决然地说一声——别了　苦难
步履如此沉重　召唤如此悠远
轻挽小桥流水　远眺大漠孤烟
新的如梦轮回　隐藏在史书的字里行间

The rivers rush forever,the strong winds circulate the ocean water to the land

Earth bulging inch by inch, the seabed is to become the mountains in a billion years

No need to ask, who knows your grand striving

No fears if success or failure is passed on or not

—Tenacious walk is taking place between heaven and earth.

February 18, 2010

江河万古奔流 劲风吹拂着海洋向大地循环

地壳寸寸隆起 海底就是亿万年后的群山

不必问 奋斗谁人知晓

何惧哉 成败是否流传

——顽强的行走 正发生在天地之间

2010 年 2 月 18 日

Land · 2020

Later, we renovated the river channel and the lake embankment
Later, we built cities and constructed buildings
Later, we liked to look up at the stars in the sky
Later, we were obsessed with crossing the oceans
Later, we investigated the particles and sub-particles
Later, we chased further the place beyond the far

Only the soil is silent, enduring alienation and oblivion
Only the seeds remain in the heart's wilderness, enduring desertion and burial
Only the weeds are wild and unruly, swaying with arrogance and blaze
Only the ravines are crisscross, carved into surges and vicissitudes
Only the unyielding old trees, brave the wind, resisting the toppling
Only a lone walker faces the setting sun, his tears blurring the scenario

土　地·2020

后来　我们整修了河道　和湖堤

后来　我们建造了城市　和楼房

后来　我们喜欢　仰望星空

后来　我们迷恋　横渡海洋

后来　我们格物粒子之下的粒子

后来　我们追逐前方以远的前方

只有泥土沉默不语　忍受着疏离　和遗忘

只有种子孤落心野　体验了冷漠　和埋藏

只有野草狂放不羁　摇曳出傲慢　和张扬

只有沟壑肆意纵横　雕刻成奔涌　和沧桑

只有不屈服的老枯树　迎风站立　抗拒倾倒

只有寂寞的独行人　面对夕阳　热泪盈眶

The point of departure was crossed, but was not left behind
The true love of gentle caress is not remembered always, but never forgotten
The time squandered has flown away, but every inch of it is eternally there
The thoughts chewed and digested, as if weeping and complaining, rise like tides
Return to an atomic particle, embracing and merging, knowing and holding each other
Reborn as the nonbeing after being, I forever stand by your side.

May 11, 2020

出发过的原点 已经越过 却未离开

轻捧着的挚爱 没有想念 不曾遗忘

挥霍过的时光 已经流逝 寸寸永恒

吐纳着的心事 如泣如诉 潮起潮涨

回归成 原子级的颗粒 相拥相融 相知相守

重生为 有之后的空无 永远站在你的身旁

2020 年 5 月 11 日

Homage

A Trilogy of Time, I

Homage to each recession of the waves
Homage to each curvature of the roads
Homage to each contraction of the hearts
Homage to each attack of the cold on the south
Homage to the courage of heroes in harm's way
Homage to the brave comeback of the lost ones

Homage to each shriveled seed
Homage to each inch of barren land
Homage to each abandoned wheel
Homage to each demolished rubble
Homage to the brilliance twinkling
Homage more to the torch that once burned

Homage to each line of verse, sincere and scalding
Homage to each hurdle, leaped over after staggering
Homage to each flower, blown away by the wind
Homage to each piece of silk, made by fair embroidering hands
Homage to meeting and understanding, to sowing and fertilizing
Homage to the passionate melody, to the silent chess game.

December 18, 2020

致　敬

——岁月三部曲之一

致敬海浪的每一次消退
致敬道路的每一个弯曲
致敬心脏的每一次收缩
致敬寒潮的每一波南袭
致敬逆行者的勇气
也致敬失落者的奋起

致敬每一粒干瘪的种子
致敬每一寸贫瘠的土地
致敬每一个废弃的车轮
致敬每一片拆除的瓦砾
致敬正闪耀的光芒
更致敬曾燃烧的火炬

致敬真诚滚烫的每一句
致敬踉跄跨越的每一级
致敬劲风吹散的每一朵
致敬素手巧绣的每一匹
致敬相遇和相知　致敬播种和孕育
礼敬激越的旋律　默敬无言的棋局

2020 年 12 月 18 日

Cold Waves

A Trilogy of Time, II

Waiting for you in snowy October on the Peak of Mount Changbai
Waiting for you in the deserted soulless Karakoram
Waiting for you in the deep ravines of Qinling Mountains
Waiting for you in Mount Everest, drifting like a speedy roadster
Standing beside me are two loyal servants
One is named Smile and the other Joy

Waiting for you on the bank of the silent and deep
Heilongjiang River
Waiting for you at Hukou Waterfall, roaring and howling
Waiting for you at the clear and gentle West Lake Bridge-head
Waiting for you in the strange and changeful depths of the ocean
I hold two heavy long swords lightly in my palms
The aged simple one is Mo Ye, the newly forged one is Fearless

Driving to you in a long car, weathered for a thousand years
Facing you with bamboo slips, hand-carved by
a Confucian scholar
Converge and collide at each twin-peak of the valley
Howl and intercept in each tumbling sea of clouds
You like your name are boundless dark tides which swallow a
thousand miles of space
I, taking the gods by the hand, am clear boldness, crossing
heaven and earth.

December 26, 2020

寒 潮

——岁月三部曲之二

在十月飞雪的长白之巅 等你
在杳无人迹的喀喇昆仑 等你
在合南纵北的秦岭深壑 等你
在漂移生长的珠穆朗玛 等你
我的身边 伫立两个忠诚的侍卫
一个叫微笑 一个叫欣喜

在静水流深的黑龙江畔 等你
在咆哮怒吼的壶口瀑布 等你
在清澈温婉的西湖桥头 等你
在波云诡谲的大洋深处 等你
我的掌心 轻握两柄厚重的长剑
古朴的是莫邪 新铸的是无惧

驾着千年沐雨的长车 驶向你
抱着儒者手刻的竹书 直面你
在每一个对耸的峡口 交汇对撞
在每一片翻滚的云海 呼啸截击
汝如其名 黑潮无际 横吞万里
吾携众神 一胆清澈 纵贯天地

2020 年 12 月 26 日

Symphony

A Trilogy of Time, III

The surging waves and the stoic banks collide
The dark gloom and the boundless warmth collide
Sudden silence and the bustling noises collide
Strong resistance and the dashing desires collide
Faith and desperation collide; recovery and loss collide
Heark! The gradually rising prologue of a grand symphony!

The compulsory duty and the fear collide
The baggage full of perseverance and the long road collide
The heroes in harm's way and the crises collide
The guarding of each door and the invasion collide
Persistence and abandonment collide; the fountainhead and the
black holes collide
Heark! The low roaring rumble of an impassioned symphony!

The armor of united strength and the contingence collide
The confident smiling eyes and the cold collide
The well-armed vastness and the isolation collide
The bustling street scenes and the emptiness collide
The commonplace and the fantastic collide;
the time and the eternity collide
Heark! The unforgettable twists and turns of
a long-standing symphony!

December 31, 2020

交　响

——岁月三部曲之三

滔天的巨浪　与坚忍的堤岸　对撞
暗色的阴郁　与无边的温暖　对撞
突然的寂静　与繁华的喧嚣　对撞
强大的阻力　与奔驰的愿望　对撞
信仰和无望对撞　复苏和失陷对撞
听　那渐起的序章　多么恢宏的交响

没有选择的担当　与恐惧　对撞
充满坚毅的行囊　与长路　对撞
一群人的逆行　与危急　对撞
每扇门的坚守　与侵袭　对撞
顽强和放弃对撞　源泉和黑洞对撞
听　那低吼的轰鸣　多么激昂的交响

众志成城的铠甲　与异变　对撞
自信微笑的眼神　与寒冷　对撞
披坚执锐的宽广　与疏离　对撞
熙熙攘攘的街景　与空旷　对撞
平凡和奇幻对撞　瞬间和永恒对撞
听　那难忘的起承转合　多么悠远的交响

2020 年 12 月 31 日

附录一·云句自选

【Appendix One】Author's Selection

那些大陆上的江河
都是我流淌的思想
Mighty rivers of those lands
Are the flowing thoughts of mine

遥不可及的遥远
银河之外的星光
The distant starlight beyond the Milky Way
O unattainable even in dreams, for which eternally I pine

那些永恒的未达啊
我们出发的原乡
Is none other than our native land—
The starting point, the finishing line.

——《银河之外的星光》（*Starlight Beyond the Milky Way*）

我有两个永恒的知音
一个在云端合掌　一个在江河裸游
一个如岩石般沉默　一个似飓风般歌唱

I have two eternal soul mates
One is lifting praying hands on the clouds
The other is swimming naked in the rivers

One is silent as a rock in the crowds

The other sings like a hurricane sending shivers

——《知音》（*Soulmates*）

合眸禅定

比遥迢更遥 比远方更远

I meditate with eyes shut

My mind reaches the farthest planet

暖意退却的季节

静静欣赏 寒潮蜿蜒向南

In a season of receding warmth

I quietly admire the cold tide winding south

——《南方以南》（*South of the South*）

渺小为 万物归元 穹间微叹

强大到 沧海一沙 从无到有

All can be as small as returning to their origin

Tiny in the vast space as a sigh

All can be as great as a grain of sand

In the boundless ocean, from nonbeing to being

双臂之间 就是时间的沙漏

Between my arms is the sand glass

——《踏海行》（*Sea Walk*）

到达是一种轻松的悲滞

出发是一种沉重的潇洒

Arrival is a kind of easy stagnation

Departure is a type of heavy elegance

就这样走走停停

万水千山已在我们脚下

I walk and stop at any station

Mountains and rivers answer with resonance

——《出发》（*Setting out*）

天地棋至中局

落子成竹在胸

Heaven and earth reach the middle game

One set piece suggests a plan well-thought

向上是任性的流动

向下是坚凝的冰晶

Upward the air flows, and carries free will

Downward the water sweeps, and becomes crystal still

——《零度的北京》（*Beijing at 0℃*）

路过了一些精灵 和众神

Passing some fairies and gods

路过了道路 和路口
路过了 那么多 路上的人
Passing roads and intersections
Passing folks — in multitudes

——《过》(*Passing*)

归来的云朵 以雨丝的身影惊艳
归来的种子 以果实的面孔斑斓
Returning clouds amaze with drizzling shadows
Returning seeds embrace with dazzling fruits

此行漫漫 魂兮归来 依旧是少年
Despite the long journey, my soul is still young and revived

——《归来》(*Return*)

用手指触碰的虚空
那是真实的真
在心灵的某个角落
那是远方的远
The emptiness my fingers touch
Is the truthfulness of truth
Somewhere in my heart
Is the distantness of distance

言即是行 行亦是言
Word is deed, and deed denotes word

——《远方》(*Afar*)

对抗逆境
最需要的 常常是意志 而不是力量
Resisting all adversities
What I need most is not strength, but will

即使面对所有的黑暗
一个人也可以进行抵抗
Facing all darkness alone
I am ready for

在犹豫与动摇的时刻
让我们坚持 而不是忧伤
In moments of hesitation and frustration
Grant us persistence, not desperation

——《抵抗》(*Resisting*)

我唇边长起的 是无尽的森林吗
我喉头突起的 是巍峨的山峦吗
Are they boundless forests that around my lips grow?
Are they towering mountains that from my Adam's apple arise?

走向朔风和白雪 走向高山和大漠
Braving wind and snow, over mountains and deserts

——《给我纤索》(*Hand Me the Towline*)

比最大 更大的重重虚妄

比最小 更小的若现若藏

The vanity greater than the greatest

The invisibility tinier than the tiniest

跨越一个维度 再次重生

拼折一个曲面 循环歌唱

Is incarnated with a new dimension of fate

Folded into a surface, singing with refrains shiny

——《真》（*Truth*）

他们 只是 在浓雾中

悄悄地 归隐

In the dense fog will they

Erase their quiet shapes

——《山脉》（*Mountain Range*）

明知终将返回地面

可我们还是要飞向蓝天

Though I eventually will be earth bound

I still aim at flying up into the blue sky

尽管压力刺痛了耳膜

飞翔依旧是最大的心愿

Though pressure sends tingling to my ear drum

Flying is still the greatest yearning I never recover from

——《起飞》（*Taking-off*）

高天的云朵
化雨 融入大地
高贵的灵魂
变土 幻为路基
Drifting clouds high in the sky
Fall as rain, permeating the earth
Noble souls from the Most High
Descend as dust, becoming roadbeds with mirth

心在最低
这最高的矗立
The lowest my heart knows
Is the topmost

站在最高处
就是把胸膛紧贴着 大地
Standing on the topmost
Is pressing my chest tightly to the ground

——《最高处》（*The Topmost*）

牵着漫漫的时间线
亿万星辰跟你走
Lead Time’s threads along
Billions of stars will follow you

牵着亿万星辰
永恒的时间 逐你奔流
Lead the billions of stars along
Eternal Time’s torrents will follow you

牵着风
云会跟你走
Lead the wind along
The clouds will follow you

——《牵》（*Lead*）

把每一次跌倒
都当成 更高站立的契机
Regard each of your fall
As a chance to stand tall

何必为自己寻找借口
要知道平庸不是平淡
Why let thousand excuses your way block
You know that mediocrity is not plainness

——《年轮》（*Growth Rings*）

我的少年时光 横跨八十年
To my youth, eighty years I assign

如果人生可以虚构
我还是放弃 所有的偶然
If life could be fictional fantasy
I will choose to give up each contingency

爱讲故事的人
讲的都是 别人的故事
Those who love to tell stories
Only tell others' stories

——《未来的往事》（*The Past of the Future*）

不在绚丽的 夕阳下 旖旎
就在轻柔的 涟漪中 归去
Either you remain in the twilight with beaming charms
Or homeward you go, in the tender ripples which part

合眸 空中有湖 闭目 怀中有你
Eyes shut, the lake in the sky; eyes closed, you in my arms

掌中有泪 心无余戚
With tears in palms, I have no fear in heart

——《湖恋》（*Lake Romance*）

成熟的树 都有一张斑驳的脸
All mature trees have dappled faces

在洁白的橡汁中加入黑色的石墨
柔韧的车轮能碾过各种路面
Instill black graphite into white oak juice
Flexible wheels can roll over any causeway

——《人间》（*The World*）

融入解冻的江河 一起奔涌

拥抱温婉的长风 北上千关

Dissolve myself into melting rivers, surging forward

Ride the mild wind, to the thousand passes northward

沉默聆听 自己一声声沉沉的心跳

那是蛰伏者积蓄已久的宣言

Listening, in silence, to my thumping heart-beat

That is the long-held declaration of the hermit

——《惊蛰》（*Awakening Insects*）

修炼 一株小草的韧性

欣赏 一颗石子的从容

I cultivate the tenacity of a blade of grass

I admire the composure of a stone

双臂 像树枝一样舞动

双脚 像树根一样坚定

My arms dance like waving branches

My feet stand firm like tree roots

——《暴风袭来的时候》（*When the Storm Rages*）

还有一种春天 就是不再期盼

只有加速奔跑 才能让时间快转

Another kind of spring needs no expecting

Quicken your running to make time spin

追上了春天 就拥抱着一起飞旋

Catch up with spring to embrace her, together whirling

只要旋得够快 就可以

永远停留在自己的春天

As long as your whirls to the high speed cling

You can always stay in your own spring

——《还有一种春天》（*Another Kind of Spring*）

我受大地母亲的重托

挥江河之笔 为你写下颂歌

By the sacred trust of Mother Earth

I wave mighty rivers, to write you an ode

我以高山父亲的名义

擎万云之笺 为你写下颂歌

By the name of Father Mount

I wave mighty clouds, to write you an ode

太阳照耀下的感恩生灵

蘸热泪之墨 为你写下颂歌

The grateful populace, bathing in the sunshine

Dip a brush into ink of tears, to write you an ode

——《颂歌》（*Ode*）

以为刚刚开始
竟然 已是七月
I deemed it a mere beginning
Already has come the month of July

以为即将结束
其实 只是七月
I deemed it an imminent ending
Actually in sight is the month of July

——《七月》（*July*）

就像孤雁倔强地昂首南飞
就像暗河的水深藏地下
Like a lone goose flying south bravely
Or the subterranean rivers deeply hidden

在最炎热的季节
向着寒冷 微笑出发
In the most scorching season
With a smile, set out, and to the cold, run

——《仲夏》（*Midsummer*）

当柴草烧尽
就把热血点燃
When the firewood is used up
ignite your blood of passion

当火光熄灭 才是最亮的温暖

When the fire burns up, it emits the brightest warmth

——《火》（*Fire*）

与千百人逆向

擦出火花四溅的激情

Going in the opposite direction of the multitudes

Produce fiery passions sparkling and flying

洒春意 重绘蓝图

转金匙 切换无言的和声

Spill the feeling of spring to re-sketch the blue print

Turn the golden keys, to switch to the soundless harmony

饮清茶 告别往事

挥酒意 化成壮丽的钟鸣

I sip the tea, bidding farewell to the past

And turning wine fervor into sounding bells

——《冬雨江城》（*River Town in Winter Rain*）

不能重生一切

那就覆盖一切

If unable to regenerate everything, then cover everything

为每一场雪 赋一首诗
赞美每一次洗礼般的倾泻
For each round of snow I compose a poem
To eulogize each down-drifting as baptismal fantasy

把阳光和阴郁的日子 全谱成悠然的音乐
Into leisurely music I turn all days gloomy or bright

——《雪》(*Snow*)

等待有一天 主人回首
把曾经的幸福 远远眺望
Until comes the day recollected by the Master
Who, from afar, fondly reflects on the past happiness

大道天行
谁知 那一刻与大阳的疏远
谁解 那欲挣脱而不得的行星之殇

That is the great Tao prevailing in heaven
Who knows the instant of aloofness from the sun?
Who knows the planets' sadness, unable the sun to shun?

——《冬日》(*Winter*)

南雁北眺 八十一磨难
九九期满 春回到羽间
In south, the geese look northward, at the eighty-one perils
At the end of the Ninth Nine, spring returns to their feathers

坚冰不喜 春意的平淡

竟因三九 恋上了严寒

The cold ice does not like the blandness of the spring season

Due to the Third Nine it falls in love with the cold of wintry weathers

——《三九》（*Third Nine*）

大阳挺立时 万物皆斑斓

When the sun stands erect, all would shine bright colors

懒散的光波 无力融解冰面

迟到的温暖 愧对整个春天

Idle light waves cannot the icy surface cleave

The late warmth feels ashamed before the whole spring

——《阳》（*Yang*）

我的无字的歌声

闪着遥远的星光

The wordless song of mine to shine

With starlight, far away, far above

——《告别时候》（*A Time for Farewell*）

春 一滴坠落的晶体

优美的流线 落入新绿

Spring, a drop of crystal falling

By a graceful line, falls into the fresh green

无奈的不舍 含泪的别离
释放的欣慰 挣脱的欢喜
Reluctant departure, teary farewell
Gratification of release, pleasure of break-free

原野不语 万花摇曳
On the silent fields shall blossoms sway

——《春谣》（*Spring Ballad*）

关于科学的科学 关于思索的思索
关于逻辑的逻辑 关于困惑的困惑
关于意义和真相的交织错落
The science of science, the thinking about thinking
The logic of logic, the confusion about confusion
Meaning and truth intersecting

把一棵树活成宇宙
闭眸观心之瞬 胸有亿万星河
Experience a universe in the life of a tree
Eyes closed, I contemplate the heart's moment,and feel in bosom a billion stars

与英雄般的小丑 同属同行
为小丑式的英雄 浅酌低歌
Both Zodiac sign and profession I share with the heroic clown
For the clownish hero, I drink a little and sing in a low voice

——《哲》（*Philosophy*）

一个当下的你 是我未来的城

这座属我的都市 正在深谷筑基

The current you is my future city

This city of mine is laying base in the valley

一个温润的人 是你壮阔的城

A modest man is a city, magnificent and grand

一杯酒 是一座城

那朵殷红的液 是城市的心

A goblet of wine is a city

The blossom of scarlet liquid is the city's heart

——《城》(*City*)

骑青牛挥别函谷关

乘木车心在列国盘桓

Riding the green bull, Lao Zi bids farewell to Hangu Pass

Riding the chariot, Confucius has his heart in the states

挥朱毫万里息烽烟

抚古琴余音珠落玉盘

Wield the brush, and beacon-fires of ten thousand li die

Play the zither, and the lingering sound is like fall of pearls on jade plates

太平洋深八千丈

华风劲吹亿万年

As deep as eight thousand feet the Pacific Ocean knows

For a billion years the strong wind of China blows

——《华风颂》（*Ode to the Wind of China*）

悠兮壮哉

那穿越了万重群山的江流浩荡

壮哉悠兮

那照耀过遥远岁月的亘古星光

Everlasting and awe-inspiring

The majestic river has winded through numerous peaks

Awe-inspiring and everlasting

The primordial starlight has illumined ancient time

——《悠兮壮哉》（*Everlasting and Awe-inspiring*）

就像落叶告别了秋树

就像雪花融进了春枝

Like falling leaves departing autumn trees, or snowflakes melting into spring branches

好似冰融化了去流浪

好似水蒸腾了去飞驰

Like ice melting to wander

Like water vaporing to fly

健行者没有心事 乐行者不妨路痴

The vigorous walker is without worries

the happy walker knows no sense of direction

——《走着》（*Walking on*）

找到几颗高温烧结的晶体

去抵抗丝丝增长的油腻

With shining pellets by the high temperature crystallized

To resist the increasing greasiness

那败而无馁的幸福

那不痛而哭的权利

The happiness of being brave after failure

The right of crying with no pain

——《致青春》（*To Youth*）

那一段无人倾听的乐曲

刻印着不朽的光辉岁月

Into the melody to which no one is listening

Are incised the immortal years of glory

扛一把石锄

把字写在石头上

On my shoulders is a stone hoe

To inscribe characters into the stone

——《光辉岁月》（*Years of Glory*）

生命是一艘船

航行就是彼岸

Life is a rowing boat

The other shore is the goal

我会再次出发

尽管脚步蹒跚

I will once again set off

Though with unsteady steps

——《走向遥远》（*Walk to the Far-off*）

真的不要怀念

那曾经青涩的美丽

真的不要追忆

那曾经挺拔的身躯

Do not miss the once immature beauty

Do not recall the once upright tree trunk

——《自述》（*Words about Myself*）

挥一只手告别黑暗

举一面旗召唤黎明

Wave a hand to bid farewell to darkness

Uphold a flag to summon up daybreak

走过的路铺满了 鲜花
要走的路正通向 险峰
Pave the roads I have already taken with fresh flowers
The roads I have chosen lead to perilous peaks

只被空中的梦想 激励
不被想象的困难 战胜
Inspired only by dreams in heaven
Never vanquished by imagined difficulties

——《人生》(*Life*)

像云一样幻化
像风一样萌动
Illusory as clouds, stirring as the wind

像一缕阳光照入平凡
此前一无所有 此后万物皆生
Like a ray of sunshine shining into the mundane
There is nothing before; there is all thriving after

——《你》(*You*)

把每一块 普普通通的砖石
都注入 为来者抗风的力量
Let each and every commonplace brick
Be infused with the comer's wind-braving strength

让每一缕 暗黑色的追逐

都留在 身后的海面上

Let each strand of dark-hued pursuit

Be left on the sea foams

——《归航》（*Voyage Home*）

是谁像无畏的大海一次次扑向月亮

是谁像高耸的山峦深情地呼唤星光

是谁像低矮的小草却紧紧地拥抱大地

是谁像永不疲倦的风儿不停地寻找自己的故乡

Who is rising toward the moon, repeatedly,

like the fearless sea

Who is calling the stars, affectionately,

like the towering mountains

Who is holding the earth tightly,

though weak as the short grass

Who is seeking homeland restlessly,

as the wind stirs the fountains

是谁相信自己

能在暴风雨中 点亮太阳

Who trusts himself

To be able to light up the sun, even against the attack of storm

——《是谁》（*Who*）

忘我 用一生去拥抱 这轻盈的飘逸

无我 每一天无限趋近 那幸福的解放

Forget Self; embrace a natural grace all with your life

Practice No-Self; approach incessantly happy liberation

学会了害怕 才是真正的生长

Learning to fear is a real growth

——《怕》(*Afraid*)

掌心的笔

是思想的刀

偶尔用于搏杀

主要用来自剖

The pen in hand

Is a sword of mind

Occasionally for fighting used

In most cases, for self-reflection

你看清了

纸上的每一个字

却读不懂 我说的话

You have seen clearly

Each word I wrote on paper

Yet cannot get the meaning

停止一切退却 准备发起冲锋

Halt all retreats, and prepare to assault

——《谏与自谏》(*Remonstration and Self-remonstration*)

将会有另一种方式
让你看清人们的面容
There will be yet another way
For you to see people's countenance gay

没有呼唤 也没有回声
三月的白桦树在静静地倾听
No calling, no echoing
March birches are quietly listening

我的心灵没有设防
也没有未化的冰层
No fortification there is in my heart
Nor is there a thick layer of unmelted ice

——《我的心灵没有设防》（*No Fortification in My Heart*）

走着的时候有道路
躺下的片段有宇 和宙
Walk and have a road ahead
Lie down and have time and space

若不在乎你
哪管你风头正劲 万众风流
If I do not love you
I care not if you are in the limelight or at the crest of charm

心中有敬畏 眼中有对手

In my heart there is awe

In my eyes there is rival

——《状态》（*State of Being*）

百年的苦斗 对抗着自己

三万个日夜 欣赏着自己

A hundred years of bitter struggle is against oneself

Thirty thousand days and nights witness my admiring

到头来 超越的人生最惬意

Eventually, a transcendental life gives most gratification

——《自己》（*Myself*）

我的祈祷如此重复 直接而简单

My prayers are in such repetitions, simple and direct

我祈祷 花谢之后仍有花开

下一个面孔 是你的笑颜

I pray after withering, the flower again opens

The next blossoming is your smiling face

——《祈祷》（*Pray*）

尊重一粒尘埃 就像敬望整个宇宙

尊重一个脚印 胜过赞美所有的繁华

Esteem a grain of dust, like looking up to the whole universe

Esteem a footprint, more than all the bustling luxuriance

尊重一棵藤的攀爬
左绕巨石 右顶粗砂
Esteem a vine's efforts to climb
Twining the boulder on the left, on the right the grits pushing

尊重一滴热泪 好似拥抱无尽的江河
尊重一场告别 仿佛重启涅槃的密码
Esteem a warm teardrop, like embracing endless lakes and rivers
Esteem a farewell, like restarting the secret codes of nirvanas

——《尊重》（*Esteem*）

把曾经的童心 再次抚摸
拂去轻尘 重新包裹
To feel, once more, my one-time childlike heart beat
Flicking away dust and wrapping it in a new disguise

被记忆唤醒的心灵
泪流满面地笑着
My heart is woken up by a memory
My cheeks were bathed in tears, my laughers were gay

——《街头突忆》（*A Flash of Memory on the Street*）

或许 真正的自由
一直就停留在 我们的心底
Perhaps, the true freedom
Is always at the bottom of our heart

——《自由》（*Freedom*）

这个美丽世界
就是这么简单
This world of beauty
Is as simple as such

你翻我 一个白眼
我回你 一个笑脸
You rolled your eyes at me
I returned with a smiling face

——《简单》（*Simplicity*）

用各种方式 证明
活过 比如书写 比如思考
With all sorts of ways, I try to prove
Having lived is like in writing or thinking

——《证明》（*Proving*）

像一个鼓鼓的气球
等人拍
重拍之后
哪管销魂 还是惊魂
Like a bulging balloon, I wait to be played
I adore beating, be the end rapture or fracture

对自己的脾气

发最后一顿脾气吧

然后乖乖睡觉

醒来后和光同尘

Lose temper to yourself, for the last time

Then go tamely to bed, and wake up blending with light or dust

——《脾气》(*Temper*)

放下了惯性 收获了新程

放下了平坦 收获了高峰

Give up inertia, and gain a prospect new

Give up plain lands, and gain the heights

赢得了战役 失去了战争

Won the battle; lost the war

变局 就在 一念之间

转身 笑拥 万千风景

The change does appear in an instant

Turn, and you witness a thousand scenes

——《变局》(*The Change*)

李白的饭局 千年未散

求醉的主角 每晚更换

Li Bai's dinner party has lasted a thousand years

The heroes willing to be drunk changed each night

只有沉默的清影
凭一点烛光 忠诚相伴
Only the wordless shadow clear and bright
Proves a loyal partner under a bit of candle light

清水小饮 闪亮的明眸
喝成 热泪盈眶的 醉眼
Drinking clear water only, sparkling eyes
Can be turned into drunken eyes, swelling with tears

——《夜宴》（*The Night Banquet*）

只有谦卑的水啊
依旧向低洼处倾泻或流淌
却充盈着所有生命的空间
Only the water, modest and humble
Towards the lowest places is still pouring or flowing
Yet all life's spaces it fills

——《谦卑之刻》（*The Moment of Humility*）

走在哪里 都是走在时光里
站在哪里 身后总有地平线
Wherever you go, you walk in time
Wherever you stand, the horizon is behind

——《时光之幻》（*The Illusion of Time*）

我明了 我晓得 我理解
但是知者不言
I see; I know; I understand
Yet he who knows does not speak

——《知者不言》(*He Who Knows Does Not Speak*)

在每一个相聚的日子 好好告个别吧
将下一次重逢 当作轮回后的初见刹那
Whenever you meet, do utter a heart-felt farewell
And regard the next reunion as the first meeting after reincarnation

——《也是生活》(*'Tis Also Life*)

几座孤峰的永恒沉默
一段江流的潇潇洒洒
Several lone peaks' eternal silence of
A section of the river's flowing elegance

和圣贤一起 仰望了星空
独对树洞 却说不出话
With saints and sages, I look up to the starry skies
Facing the tree hole, my eloquence fails

——《还是生活》(*'Tis Still Life*)

等待 风停树静的 沉谧片刻
筑一个温热的小巢 藏一条浩瀚的冰河
Waiting for the serene moment when wind dies and trees
cease hustling
I build a small, cozy nest and hide a vast flowing glacier

——《冬至·2020》（*Winter Solstice · 2020*）

把一捧心事 攥入雪球
那封印的愿望 就结晶在火热的心脉
Roll up the worry of my mind into a snowball shining
In my burning heart veins, the sealed wish is crystalizing

——《冬至·2019》（*Winter Solstice · 2019*）

你显你的潇洒 我求我的无惧
You exhibit your handsomeness; I seek my fearlessness

——《姿》（*Carriage*）

拱背 更稳地托起
最爱的你 起跳的 双足
To arch my back, more steadily uphold
Your jumping feet, my most beloved, in devotion

——《态》（*Aspect*）

生命的河 是有深度的

浅处 是静流

深处 是浩瀚

The River of Life has depth

The shallow is still flowing

The deep vast immensity

——《度》（*Degree*）

记得努力的不少 记得遗憾不多

记得的遗憾 却又无可奈何

I remember I made many efforts and had few regrets

The regrets I remember, however, I can do nothing about

——《醉》（*Drunk*）

思维扣动扳机 发射这樽张扬

My thought pulls the trigger, shooting this glass of boldness

——《醺》（*Tipsy*）

江河万古奔流 劲风吹拂着海洋向大地循环

地壳寸寸隆起 海底就是亿万年后的群山

The rivers rush forever,the strong winds circulate the ocean water to the land

Earth bulging inch by inch, the seabed is to become the mountains in a billion years

——《土地·2010》（*Land·2010*）

只有不屈服的老枯树 迎风站立 抗拒倾倒
只有寂寞的独行人 面对夕阳 热泪盈眶

Only the unyielding old trees, brave the wind, resisting the toppling
Only a lone walker faces the setting sun, his tears blurring the scenario

回归成 原子级的颗粒 相拥相融 相知相守
重生为 有之后的空无 永远站在你的身旁

Return to an atomic particle, embracing and merging, knowing and holding each other
Reborn as the nonbeing after being, I forever stand by your side

——《土地·2020》（*Land·2020*）

致敬逆行者的勇气
也致敬失落者的奋起

Homage to the courage of heroes in harm's way
Homage to the brave comeback of the lost ones

致敬正闪耀的光芒
更致敬曾燃烧的火炬

Homage to the brilliance twinkling
Homage more to the torch that once burned

——《致敬》（*Homage*）

我的掌心 轻握两柄厚重的长剑

古朴的是莫邪 新铸的是无惧

I hold two heavy long swords lightly in my palms

The aged simple one is Mo Ye, the newly forged one is Fearless

——《寒潮》（*Cold Waves*）

没有选择的担当 与恐惧 对撞

充满坚毅的行囊 与长路 对撞

The compulsory duty and the fear collide

The baggage full of perseverance and the long road collide

平凡和奇幻对撞 瞬间和永恒对撞

听 那难忘的起承转合 多么悠远的交响

The commonplace and the fantastic collide; the time and the eternity collide

Heark! The unforgettable twists and turns of a long-standing symphony

——《交响》（*Symphony*）

附录二·云诗曲谱

【Appendix Two】Music Sheets for Yun Guanqiu's Poems

作　曲：苏政

Composer：Su Zheng

云关秋诗作乐曲

银河之外的星光

只有群星，才是我的远方。
那些地球上的高山，都是我壮年的兄长。
那些大陆上的江河，都是我流淌的思想。
只有群星，才是我的远方。
那些森林和海洋，
都是我的庭院和牧场；
那些马匹还有道路，
都穿行在我的胸膛。
(间奏略)
只有
群星，才是我的远方。
遥不
可及的遥远，
银河
之外的星光，梦不能至的无垠，
那些
永恒的未达啊，我们出发的原乡。

Starlight Beyond the Milky Way

30
1.
(间奏略)
gal-lo-ping a-cross my bo - som in a line.

34
The stars a- lone are the dis- tant land of

37
mine, be-yond the Mil - ky Way, un-at-

40
tain - a- ble e-ven in dreams, for

43
which e- ter- nal- ly I pine. Is none o- ther than our na- tive

46
land. The start - ing point the fi - nish - ing line.

49
II.
coda
D.S.

七月

忽然惊觉，没有和
春天告别，竟然已是
七月。原本只期待一
抹新绿，抬头间，
浓翠目不暇接。
擦肩错过了期待已久
的季节，穿胸而过
的幻影时现时灭。拙
手缝制粗针大线的寒衣，对
将至的冷冬，孩子们浑然不觉。
以为刚刚开
始，竟然已是七
月；以为即将结
束，其实只是
七月。

July

With a start I rea-lize, I owe a fare-well to the
spring. Al-rea-dy, un-ex-pec-ted-ly, it is Ju-ly,
I had ex-pec-ted a first stroke of green. As I lift

my head, lush greens in front of my eyes ap-pear.

Nar-row-ly have I missed the long-a-wait-ed spring,

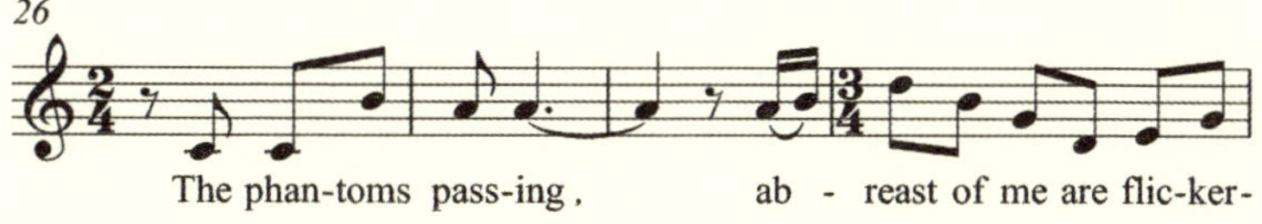
The phan-toms pass-ing, ab-reast of me are flic-ker-

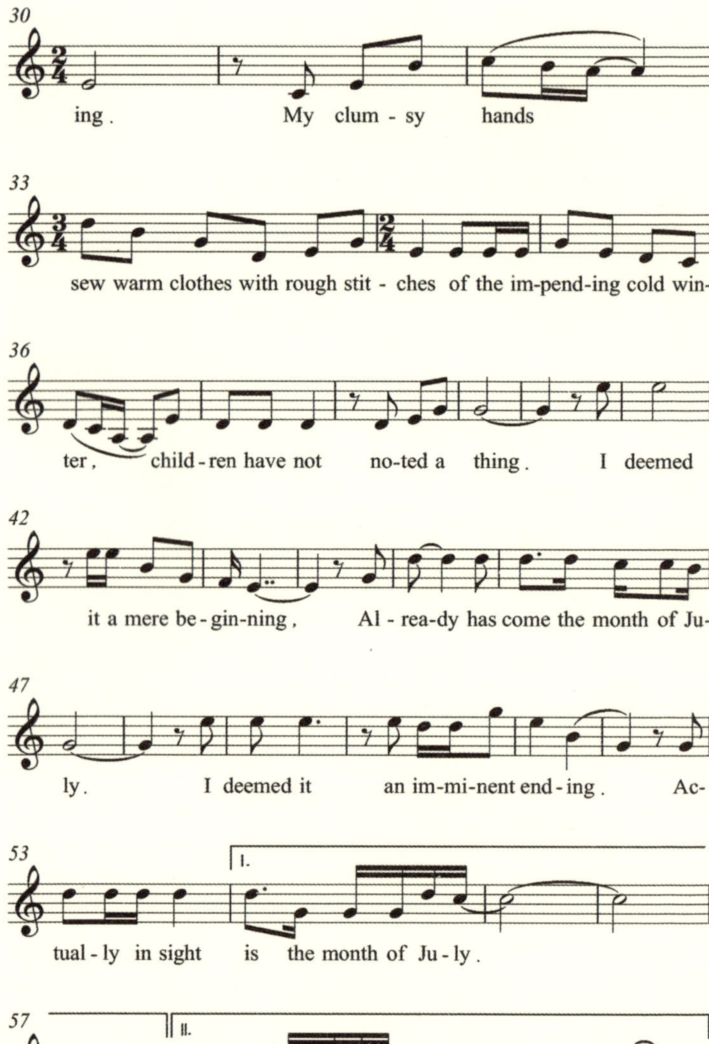
30
ing . My clum - sy hands
33
sew warm clothes with rough stit - ches of the im-pend-ing cold win-
36
ter , child - ren have not no-ted a thing . I deemed
42
it a mere be - gin-ning , Al - rea-dy has come the month of Ju-
47
ly . I deemed it an im-mi-nent end - ing . Ac-
53
tual - ly in sight is the month of Ju - ly .
57
is the month of Ju-ly .

冬雨江城

白昼 如 夜， 天 际 的 楼 宇
眉 眼 蒙 眬。 人 潮 似 水，
地 下 的 枢 纽 行 色 匆
匆。 用 亿 万 条 冷 雨 雕 琢 交 错 黏 结
的 心 境， 与 千 百 人 逆 向 擦 出 火 花 四
溅 的 激 情。 无 雪 之 都，
没 有 漫 天 寒 彻 的 冰 冷， 洒 春 意 重 绘 蓝 图，
转 金 匙 切 换 无 言 的 和 声。 冬 雨 江 城，
手 捧 彬 彬 有 礼 的 晶 莹， 饮 清 茶 告 别 往 事，
挥 洒 意 化 成 壮 丽 的 钟 鸣。
D.S.

River Town in Winter Rain

24
cold blan-ket-ing the sky. Spill the feel-ing of spring to re-sketch the
27
blue print. Turn the gold-en keys to switch to the
29
sound-less har-mo-ny. Ri-ver town in
30
win-ter rain. With crys-tal of cour-te-sy in my hand.
32
I sip the tea bid-ding fare-well to the past. And
35
I.
turn-ing wine fer-vor in-to sound-ing bells,
39
II.
turn-ing wine fer-vor in-to sound-ing bells. The snow-less ca-pi-tal
D.S.
41
结束句
turn-ing wine fer-vor in-to sound-ing bells.

华风颂

骑青牛挥别函谷关，
乘木车心在列国盘桓。
仁者非常道，诸子礼乐篇；
和气贯五洲，天地法自
然。周鼎秦砖铸风骨，唐诗宋
词谱长卷，巍峨昆仑九重山，华风劲
吹亿万年。
挥朱毫万里息烽烟，
抚古琴余音珠落玉盘。
仁者非常道，诸子礼乐篇；
和气贯五洲，天地法自
然。跨海越洋丝绸路，星移斗
转天行健，太平洋深八千丈，华风劲
吹亿万年。

Ode to the Wind of China

12
Song Ci verse un - fold in long scrolls. On the Towering
13
Kun-lun are nine peaks and heavens. For a billion years the
15
strong wind of Chi-na blo-ws.
Wield the
18
brush and the bea-con fires of ten thou-sand li die. Play the
20
zi - ther; and the lingering sou - nd is like fall - ing
21
pearls on jade plates. The ben -
22
e - vo - lent ut - ter the un - utte - ra - ble Tao; the
23
sa - ges mu - sic and ri - tuals com - pose. Har - mo - ny
24
spans five con - ti nents; Hea-ven & Earth fol-lows the

26
Self - So . A - cross seas and
27
o - ceans the Silk Roads ex - tend . The Stars move and
28
Hea - ven's vi - gor eter-nally flows . Eight thou-sand
29
feet deep the Pa - ci - fic O - cean knows . A bil - lion
30
years the strong wind of China blows . The Zhou cauldrons and the
31
Qin bricks mold Chi - na's e - thos, Tang po - e - try and
32
Song Ci verse unfold in long scrolls . On the Towering
33
Kun-lun are nine peaks and heavens. For a bil-lion years the
35
strong wind of Chi-na blows . A-cross the seas and

37
o - ceans the Silk Roads ex - tend . The Stars move and
38
Hea-ven's vi - gor etenally flows . Eight thou-sand
39
feel deep the Pa - ci - fic O-cean knows. A bil - li - on
40
years the strong wind of Chi-na blows. The Zhou cauldrons and the
41
Qin bricks mold Chi - na's e - thos , Tang poe - try and
42
Song Ci verse un-fold in long scrolls . On the Towering
43
Kun - lun are nine peaks and heavens . For a bil - lion
44
years the strong wind of China blows .

人 生

欣赏这样的人生，
握一杯茶的淡雅芬芳，
捧一席话的殷殷温情，在别
人的游戏里酣睡，在自己的沉醉中苏
醒。向往这样的
人生，因一条江的奔流筑堤，
被一朵花的绽放感动，在无
人的长街上独行，在喧嚣的殿堂里沉静。
渴望这样的
追寻这样的
人生，挥一只手告别黑
人生，聚一群鹰凌空飞
暗，举一面旗召唤黎明，
越，化一片竹破土而生，
只被空中的梦想激励，不被想象的困难
走过的路铺满了鲜花，要走的路正通向
战胜。
险峰。
走过的路铺满
D.S.
了鲜花，要走的路正通向险峰。

Life

6
10
13
16
21
25
I ad-mi-re this kind of life. Breathe
the scent of a cup of tea in hand.
Hold the warmth of a con-ver-sa-tion in palms.
Slum-ber in the games of o-thers. A-wa-ken in my own deep
in-to-xi-ca-tion. I yearn for this kind of
life. Build an em-bank-ment due to a ri-ver's tor-rents.
Feel moved due to a flo-wer's blos-som, Walk

29
a-lone in the long emp - ty a-ve-nue. Think qui-et in the cla-mo-rous
32
pa - lace. I de-sire this kind of life.
38
Wave a hand to bid fare - well to dark-ness. Up-
43
hold one flag to sum-mon up day-break. Ins - pir-ed on - ly by
47
dreams in hea-ven. Ne - ver van-quished by
49
I.
i - ma - gined dif - fi - cul - ties,
52
II.
i-ma-gined dif-fi-cul - ties I seek
57
this kind of life. Ga-ther

60
a flock of ea - gles to tra - verse the o - pen sky .
63
Be a grove of bam-boos to break through the so- il . Pave
67
the roads I have al - rea - dy ta - ken with flo - wers .
69
The roads I have cho-sen lead to pe - ri - lous peaks .
73
Pave the roads I have al - rea - dy ta - ken with flo-wers .
76
The roads I have cho - sen lead to pe - ri -
78
lous peaks .

夜 宴

李白老师策　划　了　一　个　人　的　夜　宴，
邀　了　明　月　又　请　了
清　影。　只　是　不　知
有　几　瓮　残　酒，　几　双　竹　筷，
几　副　杯　盘。
有　酒　之　席，　一　个　人
的　饭　局　能　吃　成　一　万　人　的
盛　宴；
无　酒　独　酌，　清　水　小　饮　闪
亮　的　明　眸　喝　成　热　泪　盈
眶　的　醉　眼。　李
白　的　饭　局　千　年　未
散，　求　醉　的　主　角　每　晚
更　换，　作　陪　的　明　月　随　心
出　现，　只　有　沉　默　的
清　影，　凭　一　点　烛　光
忠　诚　相　伴。
D.S.

The Night Banquet

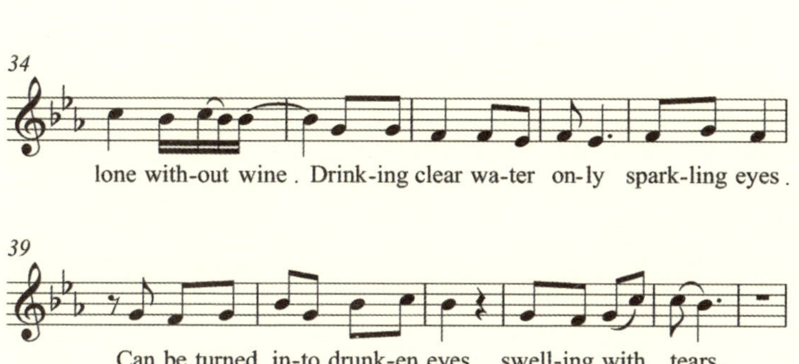
34
lone with-out wine . Drink-ing clear wa-ter on-ly spark-ling eyes .
39
Can be turned in-to drunk-en eyes swell-ing with tears .

45
Li Bai's din-ner par-ty has last-ed a

50
thou-sand years . The he-roes will-ing to be drunk changed

54
each night. The ac-compa-nying bright moon as wished

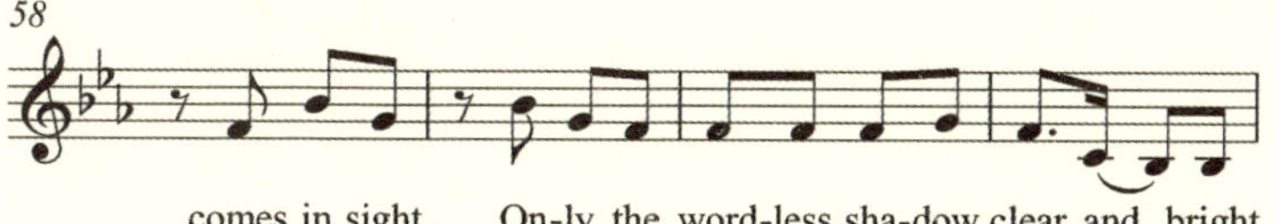
58
comes in sight . On-ly the word-less sha-dow clear and bright .

62
1.
Proves a lo-yal part-ner un-der a bit of can-dle

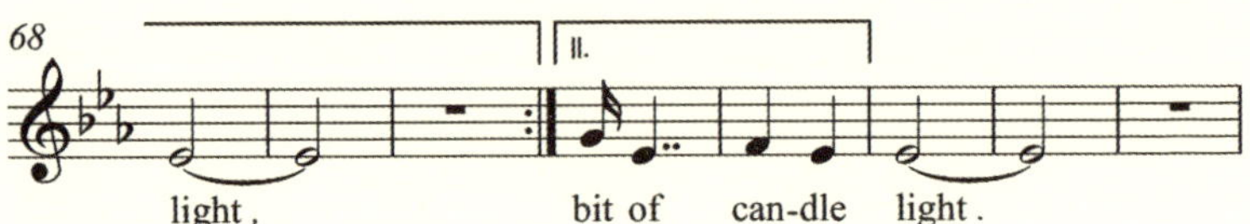
68
II.
light, bit of can-dle light.

76
Li Bai's din-ner par-ty has last-ed a

81
thou-sand years. The he-roes will-ing to be drunk changed

85
each night, drink-ing alone with-out wine. Drink-ing clear wa-ter

89
on-ly spark-ling eyes. Can be turned in-to drunk-en

94
eyes swell-ing with tears.

译者简介

About the Translators

张剑 教授，北京外国语大学英语学院院长、博士生导师、著名英语文学与文化翻译、研究专家。

Zhang Jian, dean and professor at School of English, Beijing Foreign Studies University; translator and expert on English literature and culture.

赵冬 博士，北京外国语大学副教授，英语文学和文化研究学者。

Dr. Zhao Dong, Associate Professor of English at Beijing Foreign Studies University; scholar of English literature and cultural studies.